FEVER
UNCOMMON WORLD

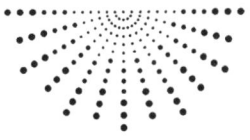

ALISHA KLAPHEKE

This story follows *Waters of Salt and Sin* and precedes *Plains of Sand and Steel* and *Forest of Silver and Secrets*

For my husband, who heals me everyday

This is a work of fiction. All events, dialogue, and characters are products of the author's imagination. In all respects, any resemblance to persons living or dead is entirely coincidental.

Text copyright © 2017 by Alisha Klapheke
Cover art copyright © 2017 by Merilliza Chan
Typography by Angela Fristoe

All rights reserved.
Visit Alisha on the web! alishaklapheke.com

Library of Congress Cataloging-in-Publication Data
Klapheke, Alisha
Fever/Alisha Klapheke. —First edition.
Summary: As the son of affluent Old Farm's chairman, Calev brings the agreement between their people and the Empire's local ruler to the capitol city for approval to avoid war, but when he is robbed and learns his beloved Kinneret is dying, his errand twists into a living nightmare.
ISBN 978-0-9987379-2-8 **(ebook)**
ISBN 978-0-9987379-5-9 **(print)**
[1. Fantasy. 2. Magic—Fiction.] I. Title.

Printed in the United States of America
10 9 8 7 6 5 4 3 2 1
First Edition

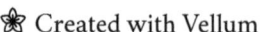
 Created with Vellum

1
CALEV

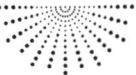

Readying to meet the ruler of the most powerful Empire in the world wasn't a simple task. Especially when he held my dreams in his very spoiled and reportedly vicious hands.

Although my home, Old Farm, sat inside the Empire, we were nothing like the kyros's court. Where we had democratic meetings and long days in the sun, they had a tight-fisted tyrant and deeply dyed tent walls of the finest fabrics to keep them cool on even the hottest months.

Seven horses and more colored packs than I could tally crowded the beaten earth in front of our Old Farm community building. I tied my own pack onto my mount and ran a hand down the mare's neck.

"This is going to be a long ride," I whispered into the coarse, braids of her mane. "At least compared to our usual jaunts around the fields and hills. I'll make sure you have plenty of water and I just happened to nab three of the finest apples on the Broken Coast for you."

Despite my misgivings about the new kyros and his lack of respect for human life, I couldn't wait to see the capitol again. It was a city of tents supported by tall towers and surrounded by a huge wall of stone. There would be sights and sounds there we never saw in Jakobden or Old Farm.

It'd been years since I'd visited, and I buzzed with excitement, thinking of how they would receive me at the fine court there. I was finally of age and they would treat me properly. I might even find the courage to suggest even more changes in the caste system in order to aid those who had once been low-caste like Kinneret and her sister Avigail. Politics and social situations were my strength and I would prove it even more with this quest.

My horse snuffled against my chest as my father walked up behind me.

"Son, are you quite certain you know how to behave in the kyros's court? Full names are required. You can't just think up some wild idea and present it while you're there. Focus on gaining Kyros Meric's mark on the agreement between us and our new amir, Ekrem. Nothing else matters."

"I know." I fought the urge to roll my eyes skyward. He'd only told me the requirements about two thousand times.

Eleazar kicked his horse gently and walked him over. "Brother, I think you should consider asking Ezra to come with us. He has had three audiences with this new kyros. He says the man is...less than kind."

I put my foot in my stirrup and threw a leg over my mare, frustration making my movements a bit more forceful than was absolutely necessary.

"Ezra has work here," I said. "I can handle this. And we have all the protection we need with Serhat and the others coming along." I smiled at the tall, fair-haired fighter.

Serhat nodded as she attempted to steer her horse toward us. She was better on a boat than on a steed. But at least she knew her way around a yatagan. The road to the Empire's capitol was teeming with thieves and the city itself was known to have its rough spots.

Thinking of boats brought Kinneret to mind. Not that she was ever far from my thoughts these days.

"Kinneret said she'd see us off." I held up a hand to block the sun's increasing light, hoping to catch her strolling toward me with those hips of hers.

A group of men and women walked down the road that led to the docks, but none of them had Kinneret's wild hair or the bounce in their step like her. I hoped everything was all right. I'd heard of several people in town who'd come down with a fever. Surely she wouldn't get it. Sicknesses never touched her.

"You don't have the sun to wait on her. If you are going, you must go now." Father handed me a rolled parchment. "This is the agreement. It is the most important item you've ever held, son. If you lose it, if it falls into the wrong hands, our entire culture may cease to exist. Amir Ekrem is a patient man and a kind ruler for our region, but his actions are influenced by Kyros Meric, who seems to never have heard of the word kindness. Do not fail Old Farm, my son. If you do, there is no way the council will permit you to become the next chairman. And I would have to agree."

My tunic rode up against my neck, and I tugged it loose. "I know, Father. You've told me this again and again." He frowned, so I touched his shoulder as I leaned down from my mount. "I promise I will make you proud."

A rare smile beamed from Father's bearded face. He patted my hand with his calloused fingers. "You already have. I am blessed with two sons who are very fine indeed."

Eleazar mumbled something from his saddle.

Father spun. "What was that?"

"Nothing," Eleazar said. "Shouldn't we go now? Or do you need ten more minutes with your beloved Calev?"

Father glared, eliciting a murmured apology from Eleazar. My brother was going to be a real treat on this ride to Akhayma.

With the agreement safely in my pouch, I rode up to Serhat. She was looking a bit paler than normal. "You feeling all right?"

She swallowed and straightened her back. "Yes, Calev ben Y'hoshua. I am perfectly fit for this mission."

Her red leather vest was immaculate except for one deep cut on her left shoulder. She'd nearly lost her head during the battle at Quarry Isle when we'd fought to free Avi from that awful place. I wondered if she kept the damaged vest to remind herself that she'd bested Death. It seemed like something she would do. The amir's fighters were such an interesting blend of pride and humility, and Serhat was a prime example, though right now she looked in need of another night's sleep. She wiped her eye and pressed her hand against her mouth.

"Don't get sick on me now. I need you on that mount and ready to fight." Several townsfolk had fallen ill with a bad fever.

Serhat untied her water from her saddlebags and drank down three, big swallows. "Just thirsty. I am well. Don't worry." Her thin lips lifted at one side.

"Good. I don't think I'd enjoy hoisting you back onto that elephant you're calling a horse."

Her quiet laugh followed me as I trotted closer to the road. I looked longingly toward Kinneret's new home near the docks, wishing I had the sun to wait on her. But she would understand my leaving, and I'd be back quickly.

Tucking my worries away, I kicked my mare into a gallop and led the party toward the hills that rolled inland.

WE CROSSED the mercurial river that through the Empire, past Silvania's deep forests, and onward to the Great Expanse that led to the far West. We were making good progress, but by the time we reined in our mounts at an inn, Serhat looked like a corpse. And the rest of my party didn't look much better.

An inn worker—a tall girl in thick braids—took my mare and held a hand out for the others' reins.

Serhat listed left, then fell from her saddle.

I hurried to her side, Eleazar on my heels.

She was clearly disoriented, blinking and gasping. I put a hand on her head. Heat blazed from her clammy skin.

I sat back. This was awful. "She has the fever."

Eleazar sighed. "I do too."

"What?"

My brother nodded sadly and swallowed. I hit my thigh with a fist as the inn's front door swung open. Why did this sickness have to hit now? A man wearing the dirtiest apron ever strolled out.

"What's this?"

Eleazar and I helped Serhat to her feet as the others

dismounted and handed their horses to the girl with the braids. Eleazar panted with the effort to keep Serhat standing.

I adjusted my pack, making sure the agreement was still there and safe. "We need lodging for the night, please. And I think most of my party here is ill."

Kinneret would've lied a tiny bit just to be sure the man wasn't afraid of contracting our illness. I hated lying. I was terrible at it. But I had to make certain everyone was safe. We couldn't sit out here in the street all night, open to thieves and cutpurses.

Swallowing my values, I lied to the best of my ability. "The rest of these men and women ate some bad meat. I had abstained for purity reasons."

Eleazar eyed me, but kept quiet.

The innkeeper wiped his massive hands on his apron. "All right then. Let's get them all inside to puke and be done with it. I am a merciful man, but I will insist on a twenty percent increase on my usual fees."

Eleazar's mouth fell open. Sweat beaded along his red-bronze headtie. "That is not good business."

I touched his sleeve and looked the innkeeper in the eye. "We will pay fifteen more than the last time our people stayed here."

Ezra had told me how much to pay. He'd been up this way to speak with a group of Silvanians that claimed they'd spotted a group of Invader scouts not far from the capitol.

The innkeeper scowled, then stuck out a hand for me to shake.

The inside of the establishment was nothing to crow about. A sad fire on the far side cooked a large bird and four dented tables held a crowd of Silvanian merchants, Empire fighters on patrol, and two families with more children than I could count.

Once Eleazar and I were settled in the best room, Serhat being just one door down, my brother collapsed onto the bedding.

"I'm going to have to leave without you all in the morning," I said.

I didn't want to. It would be dangerous traveling alone to the capitol and even inside the city walls, but this agreement couldn't wait. If we allowed too much sun between the conclusion of the last agreement and the new one, Kyros Meric might think of all sorts of additions that would hurt Old Farm. Amir Ekrem, a friend, would fight them, but he could only do so much without risking his position and his life.

"I know." Eleazar wheezed.

I gave him a cup of questionable water before sending off a letter to Father about the illness. The inn's rock dove took off with the message securely bound to its leg before the sun set.

"He'll want you to wait for him." Eleazar's hand drifted toward the side table, but the cup fell from his hand.

My throat tightened. He was truly sick. This wasn't like him at all. I cleaned the water with a folded rag, then did my best to get a night's sleep. I had to rise before anyone and ride on. I couldn't let my father stop me due to this fever. He'd never give me this opportunity again and I couldn't stand the thought of failing him and disappointing Kinneret with my lack of political skills.

Tomorrow, I would ride like the wind.

2
AVI

The door to my new house was the brightest blue. We'd bought the place right after our bell removal and our rise to high-caste, and Kinneret had let me choose the azure color. I'd picked the hue to match Oron's glass gaming pieces although Kinneret thought I'd selected the shade to echo her beloved sea.

I pushed the lovely blue door open and saw my sister at the table. She stared at a map of the Pass, the new ports she'd marked dotting the jagged coastline.

"Aren't you supposed to be seeing Calev off before his trip to court?" I set my shipping schedule beside her elbow. "Eh. Kinneret. What is wrong?"

She shook her head, then looked up at me with glazed eyes. "Oh. I'm not feeling well." Her fingers dragged over the map, smearing a row of black circles.

"Kin?"

She slid from her chair and tumbled to the stone floor, her head knocking the wooden flooring.

My heart seized.

Tossing the chair aside, I took her by the arms and cradled her head in my lap. Her forehead was hot as the decking at midday.

She blinked and moved her chin as if she was recovering from being hit in the jaw. "I'm fine. I just forgot about Calev's trip. I'll go now."

"Oh no you don't."

I heaved her up and walked her to the bed. Easing her down, my skin pressed against hers. She was absolutely burning up. My mind whirled. This couldn't be the fever that had killed the sailmaker's son, could it? He was a horrible person, but no one deserved to die like that. There were more who had the same type of illness in the merchant's quarter in town.

"I'll be fine," Kinneret croaked.

Then a memory crashed through my mind. My parents side by side on the bed, their cheeks bright red. I could still smell the sickness.

"I'll be fine," my mother had said.

And she'd died the very next morning.

Now, I dabbed a wet cloth over Kinneret's flushed face. She didn't seem to notice the attention.

Panic climbed my chest and choked me. "I'll be right back, sister. Don't get up."

I rushed out of the door, sprinting past the sailors on their way to their ships and weaving between women and children on the path into town. Old Farm wasn't far. Maybe I could catch Calev before he left for Akhayma, and he could come and pray for Kinneret and be her luck and get her well again. He had a special link with Kinneret. He would save her, and I wouldn't lose her like I'd lost Mother and Father.

The Old Farm courtyard was empty except for a few men talking over a list of some kind.

"Where is Calev ben Y'hoshua? Did he already leave? It's an emergency."

"Avigail Raza." The closest man smiled. "I'm sorry, but yes, you missed him. Is there anything we can do?"

"My sister. She has a fever."

They traded glances. "We have a healer here. Would you like us to call him?"

"Please." I smiled in thanks for their offer, but I had no real hope for this. The sailmaker's son had seen a healer, and he'd died all the same. "Have you heard about anyone else that has this sickness?"

The man frowned. "Sadly, yes. Five more fell sick in town. None here yet. Two of the townsfolk have moved into the next life."

I made the sign of the Fire on my forehead as a ringing sounded in my ears.

Kinneret was not allowed to die.

I needed her here. I wasn't ready to be on my own and the world was a better place with her in it. She'd worked hard to end much of the low-castes' suffering. It was her that petitioned to end Outcasting. None had been subjected to it since. She had more to do in this life.

"Are you all right? You aren't becoming ill, too, are you?" the man asked.

"No. Please send your healer to Kinneret Raza's house at the docks."

"We will do it immediately."

I didn't wait for their bows and kind words. Maybe Oron knew which route Calev was taking to the capitol. Maybe I could follow him and get him back here before it was too late.

Oron was on our old boat, rolling up the sail. On his free days, he always went out on his own. He said he had ghosts to conquer, whatever that meant.

When I told him about Kinneret, he dropped the sail and raced to our house.

∼

BY THE TIME the sun was down and the Old Farm healer had left, Oron was as panicked as me. He paced the floor at Kinneret's feet, the sound of his soft steps mixing with the shushing of the Pass beyond the docks.

I knelt beside the bed and brushed my older sister's hair away from her sticky cheeks. "I'm going after Calev," I said quietly so I wouldn't disturb her rest. "He can heal her."

Oron set his hand on the back of my head. "Avi." The oil lamp hanging from the ceiling cast flickers of light across his face. "Calev isn't a healer. Our girl will heal on her own or she won't. That's that."

I shoved his hand away and stood. Studying his eyes, I could see he would keep repeating this if I pushed my plan to go after Calev. The healer, Ekrem, and Calev's father had thought I was delusional when they heard my idea to bring Calev back to heal her.

Well, I wasn't about to just sit here and do nothing.

I was Kinneret Raza's sister and we didn't understand the words *give up*.

Ekrem, Oron, Calev's father, and the healer were all wrong.

Calev could give Kinneret strength enough to heal. And I would prove it and save my sister. She'd risked her life for me not long ago, and by the Fire, I would do the exact same for her.

When deep night poured over Jakobden, I leaned close to Kinneret's ear. Her chest moved slowly, too slowly, up and down.

"I will bring him back for you, Sister."

I wanted to cry over her, to beg her to wake up and heal herself, but I was too old for that now. I knew it would do no good.

So after a gentle squeeze of her limp hand, I slipped past Oron's sleeping form in the other bed and ghosted out the door.

I didn't care what dangers lurked in the Empire's capitol. I would go there and find Calev before Death could grip my family again.

3

CALEV

Night dropped like an axe as I galloped across the desert plains. At home on Old Farm, the sun danced toward the horizon and gave us time to tuck our scythes away in the barns and wash our hands for the blessing. But here, just outside the Empire's capitol city of Akhayma, the arid plateaus to the West cut off the sun's brutal heat, leaving only cold and shadows as I rode up to the city gates.

I smiled into the darkness, almost wanting to laugh. I'd made it, even though there'd been so many problems. I was here and nearly finished with my duty. Kinneret and Father were going to be so proud. This would prove I was ready to become Chairman of Old Farm. Soon, I'd have the position to take care of Kinneret, not that she needed me, and to hold my head high.

Hopefully, Eleazar, Serhat, and the rest would join me soon. I'd made sure a healer was paid to visit them while I was gone. They were strong. They'd get through this illness.

At the gate, guards armed with poles and sheathed yatagans gave me a once-over, then waved me through the stone arch and into the moonlit city.

Covering the bubbling canals, tents tied to tall, skinny towers rippled like sails between masts. Cinnamon, wine, peppers, heated metal—the air here held nothing of home. The last time I'd been here—years ago—I'd ridden behind Father on his mount, my fingers digging into his sash to keep from toppling from the saddle as I strained to see it all.

I reined my horse in and patted my pack gently, reassuring myself. The edges of Amir Ekrem and my father's agreement—a delicate promise between two very different cultures—pressed into the soft leather. All I had to do was get a good night's rest, then present the document to the kyros in the morning for his approval. Old Farm needed this agreement with Jakobden's amir to remain secure. Without it, the Empire could do as they liked with my people and their lands.

I swallowed. I only hoped Kyros Meric would continue to support the treaty. Amir Ekrem did, but I would have to remind the kyros that we grew valuable barley and rare lemons like no other farm could.

Laughter tumbled out from a path leading south through the maze of streets. I followed the sound of rolling dice and the smell of minted, roasted lamb. The path between the tents that ran along the waterways wound its way under a row of signs hanging over doorways. I knew enough desert tongue to read the word *inn* below a painting of an egret. Out front, a boy—too old to be missing teeth but missing them all the same—took my horse and one of my silver coins.

"I'll need her back at dawn," I said.

Normally at this time of the evening, I'd be chasing after Kinneret. My face heated at the thought of the night before I'd left. We needed to marry before I died of want for her. She was so busy during the day working on Amir Ekrem's full ship and retooling Jakobden's fleet that we didn't see one another nearly often enough.

Just inside the inn's open door, a woman, wearing a dark kaftan, smiled from where she sat on a tall stool. She stood and reached for my pack.

"You need a place to stay, my lord? Why are you on your own? Where's your fine retinue?" Her accent opened the trade tongue vowel sounds as she commented on my embroidered clothing.

"I'm from Jakobden. Old Farm. There's a bad fever. Some of my retinue are sick at home and the rest are now recovering at inns along the route."

The last person I'd checked on before leaving was Serhat. The innkeeper's daughter had been mopping her blond hair with a wet cloth.

"I do need a room, please," I said. "But I'll keep my things, thank you."

One of the men seated around a green and red gaming table mumbled a slur about Old Farm men and virility that pinched at my good mood.

I eyed the man, grabbed the hem of my tunic, and shook it, lifting it just a little. "It's not true, good man, but if you'd like to check yourself…"

Being around Oron had definitely changed me. Kinneret's first mate, a wine-loving man from the Northern Isles, never missed an opportunity to shock people with jokes you laughed at but probably shouldn't. Before I knew him, I would've ignored the stranger's bawdy slur and probably blushed like a fool. Oron's influence had washed some of the innocence off me and made me bold.

The insulter said something that was surely swearing, but his friends laughed good-naturedly as the woman led me through the crowded room.

The room for rent was a slice of space and a hammock between two walls of striped wool. Not the best accommodations. But my legs ached and my stomach roared with hunger. This would be good enough. I started to set my pack in the corner, then turned to the woman.

"What do people here do about stealing?"

"Thieves lose a hand. No exceptions. Not a lot of stealing going on."

"Well, all right then." I'd still keep the agreement in my sash. I wasn't going to be separated from it any second of any day.

The parchment was smooth under my fingertips as I unrolled it a fraction. My father's name, inked in dramatic calligraphy, tossed a smile over my lips. The entire top third of the agreement lay blank and ready for the kyros's sigil and name. I wondered what type of brush or quill his scribe would use to create the colorful rendering of *Kyros Meric, the Eternally Victorious*.

With the agreement tucked away behind the silk and linen pomegranates embroidered on my sash, I sat at an empty table in the main room.

"I am Samira, not that you asked." The innkeeper's smile held a touch of mockery. "What can I get you?"

I ignored her less-then-respectful tone and soon my

stomach was full of lamb, flatbread, and honeyed dates speckled with some herb that was familiar, but I couldn't place. The room blurred, and my sore muscles eased a little bit. I decided to play some cards.

~

I COULDN'T UNDERSTAND the first punch. What it was. What it meant for me.

I'd just come out of the inn to catch my breath, to try to clear my head of the wine I'd stupidly gulped too much of during the card game. The lotus tower holding up the tents in the area cooled my palm, then my cheek as I leaned into it and tried to stop the world from spinning. I couldn't remember how long I'd walked. Why had I done this to myself? I was smarter than this.

But was this just from wine?

My thoughts were foggy. My head was going to hurt badly during my audience with the kyros tomorrow. I pressed my back into the tower and the moon eyed me disdainfully.

"You're right, moon. Wine is never worth the headache."

Some men walked out of the inn, laughing, and started down the road, their arms thrown over one another's shoulders. It was late. Maybe they could walk back with me, make sure I didn't further ruin my reputation.

I took a step toward them. The wooden signs, marking each establishment, blurred in my hazy eyes, white paint looking wet and dripping. Then they disappeared into the night.

A stranger came up on me fast.

When knuckles crashed against my skull and my headtie

slipped over one eye, I was equally as surprised as the chicken who took the brunt of my collapse into her nesting spot beside the tower. The part of my mind that didn't seem to care about my possible death begged the question: Why was it always chickens? Chickens in Kurakia last time. Chickens here now. They dogged me like awkward ghosts, haunting my every misadventure.

I shook my foggy head, ignoring a disgruntled *squawk* coming from behind me, and—hoping to hide the agreement from my attacker—I rolled, keeping it under my back, but still in my sash.

A man with a ragged beard laughed. The same man that had been playing cards with me earlier? Another? He kicked me in the stomach.

My breath blasted out of me. My lungs couldn't grab any air. I was going to vomit.

Gasping, I held up my hands and lifted a foot to push him away. But he had friends. Two of them. One had definitely been at the inn. I recognized him. Another kick came, this time to my knee. Pain spidered up my leg.

A fist launched into my face. As heat that would eventually become pain seared my nose, I grabbed for a sleeve of one of the men and missed.

"What's in your sash there, *bather*?" The man slipped fingers under the knot and tugged. "I knew one of you rich Old Farm's once. Think you're better than the rest of us."

Bather. A slur that mocked my people's holy cleansing ritual.

I forced my fingers to stay away from the agreement. It pressed against my spine. "No, we don't. And I have no money. Spent it all on food and wine."

"Sounds like our plan, Behir," the second man said.

"Yeah, but the *bather* still has something in that fancy sash of his."

"I told you I spent it all on dinner."

"And all that gray plant too." The bearded man elbowed the man next to him.

"Gray plant?" I mumbled through the pain. They weren't making sense. I hadn't bought any of that.

Then I realized what had happened. The bits of herb sprinkled over my honeyed dates—it had been gray plant. A full leaf of that foul plant could put a horse to dreaming. I looked up at my attackers realizing they'd planned this robbery. Had the innkeeper known about it too? Had she been in on it?

They laughed as I tried to get to my knees. Maybe I could run off. Find a dark alley to hide in. Blood streamed from my nose, hot and deserved for all my foolish actions.

"You have something in there, don't you? Tell us the truth, Old Farm," the first attacker spat.

I couldn't lose the parchment. Father would banish me. Well, maybe not banish me, but close to it. I'd be humiliated in front of everyone. Before Ekrem became the amir, it would've meant war. Now it meant tense negotiations that would set back the harvest. Without the agreement, the peace between Old Farm and the kyros and amir could be ruined.

I had to think. I had to think quickly like Kinneret.

I tried to smile even though my face felt like a road at midday—trampled and far too hot.

"Fine," I said. "I lied."

They traded a look. The third man popped his knuckles.

Swallowing, I slid my coin purse out of my sash and opened it up, showing the coin I had for the trip home.

Would the kyros help me get back if I didn't have a silver

piece to my name? If he didn't, I'd be stuck here until I could work my way to affording water and food for the return journey. I'd be late, far, far behind schedule. Father and Ekrem would send messengers. There'd be misunderstandings. Dangerous misunderstandings if I went missing.

"I have a little left." I closed the bag and held it out. "Take it. Enjoy a meal on me." I turned to spit blood out of my mouth, the sudden movement making my nose flame.

The ragged-bearded man clapped his skinny hands. "This one is pretty funny." He snatched the purse and tucked it into his sash.

His friend kicked my leg out from under me. I fell again, the night still spinning like the string toy Kinneret's sister, Avi, loved when she was little.

"I still want what you're hiding in your sash. That parchment." He looked at his friend. "He's funny and funny means clever. That writing could be the deed to a fine horse. Or a note on silver owed. Could be worth a lot. He wants us to leave and there has to be a reason he'd give up that coin so quick."

Quick? They'd all but beaten my nose in. I fought panic, wrestled it into the back of my mind. "Only because I have an Intended at home who'd prefer my face intact enough to shower her with praise."

The last punch was a surprise too.

It hit like a horse's hoof to my head.

I woke up lying on my side, head pounding, with the sun stretching over the sandy earth to shoot me in the eye.

Sitting up, I touched my shoulder, my back, and the gritty road under me.

They'd stolen the agreement. A cold sweat rolled down my

neck. My reputation would be ruined before it had a chance to be born. I'd never get the chairman position. Kinneret would be a fool to wed me and she was no fool. I couldn't stop imagining the furrow between her eyebrows and the sound of Father scolding me.

4
AVI

Blinking tears away, I smacked the horse's flank and she sped up, hooves roaring over the clumps of scrub and dusty earth. My legs quivered. I'd never ridden so far. At least I was better at it than Kinneret. My sister ruled on the water, but on a horse's back, she wasn't worth much. I'd taken right to riding when Calev first let me try at Old Farm.

I swallowed. I had to get them together again before Kinneret burned away like Mother and Father.

Tears blurred the sight of a family with a loaded down camel. Grain traders led a massive six-wheeled cart pulled by braying ox-lions. A band of colorfully dressed entertainers looked more likely to pick the coins from my sash than make me laugh. I wiped the wetness from my cheeks.

Crying wouldn't keep Kinneret from dying. Calev's love might. I had to get to him. Now.

The Empire's capitol loomed in the distance like a rogue

wave ready to crash over all of us down here on the wide and sandy road.

Calev would believe me. He'd believe Kinneret would get better if he came home to her. All the rest of them thought I was a madwoman. But Oron, Ekrem, and Chairman Y'hoshua would wake to find Calev's second best horse and me gone, and know I was a *smart* madwoman.

Inside Akhayma's walls, I ignored the bizarre tents and wild smells—both pleasant and rank—of the city as I pushed through the crowd.

"Come on, Arrow."

Sweat matted the mare's sinuous neck. I moved toward one of the waterways that streamed under the tented pathways. She lowered her head to drink and the dawn's light skirted over her dusty mane. She and I both would need nine baths after this horrible trip.

A man shouted at me in some foreign language, then switched to my own—what they called the trade or common tongue. "Stop." He shook a fist at me and jerked Arrow's reins out of my hand.

I ripped them out of his fingers. "Back off."

"The signs." He pointed at a tiny, wooden square covered in five languages. *No drinking from the canals. Cups only, please.*

"I don't have a cup. This is ridiculous."

The man kept jabbering on at me in his language and mine. There weren't any bowls anywhere. How did they expect travelers to water their horses? There had to be containers to use somewhere—

Crockery crowded a booth set up beside the main thoroughfare. I dragged Arrow away from her drink and pointed to a tiny bowl in front of the merchant. "Could I use this? Just for a second? I'll bring it right back."

The thin-faced woman shook her head. "No. Buy only."

I looked to the sky. "Fine." I gave her the coins and finally my poor mount had a good drink and me along with her.

I eyed the man who'd shouted at me. His long-sleeved, coat-tunic bore an emblem with a thick, blue line and a sun. "Are you in charge of the water?"

Crossing his arms proudly, the man smiled.

I had to grin at his transformation. "You really should have a larger sign at the front gate. One that details exactly what visitors are supposed to do. It would keep the shouting down."

His face fell, and his arms dropped to his sides. "You, a little girl, offer me advice?"

I splashed some water on Arrow's neck. "I'm fifteen and then some." Since the horrors of Quarry Isle, I felt like I was more like ninety-years-old. "Now, where do I go to see someone who has a meeting with the kyros and his scribe?"

Blinking, the man stuttered, "You'd go to the Kyros Walls and present yourself." He waved toward a narrower path cobbled in reddish stone.

"Thank you," I said, heading off. I'd wasted enough time.

If Kinneret's condition worsened…no, I wouldn't think about it. It didn't do any good to thrash around and cry. I had to focus on finding Calev. His calm head and his heart for my sister—that was what would fix everything. Kinneret was right; Calev was luck made real.

AT THE KYROS WALLS, a guard with a dark red beard stopped me.

"Appointment with the lower bench?" he said in accented trade tongue.

"No. But my friend has an appointment with the kyros and—"

He snorted. "Move on, girl."

It was all I could do not to ram my heels into my mare and trample the idiot. I breathed out my nose and nudged my horse forward, just a step.

"You misunderstand, good man. My friend is Calev ben Y'hoshua, son of the chairman of Old Farm in Jakobden and sent here by Amir Ekrem to approve an agreement."

The guard across the way tugged his helmet off and his sweat-slicked black hair held the shape of the metal. He took hold of my reins. "Like he said, move on. Before you get into trouble with your stories."

"It's not a story. It is the truth. And you will be punished if the kyros learns you were the reason his new amir in Jakobden failed to uphold a truce lasting centuries!"

I wasn't totally sure all of that was true, but it sounded good.

Suddenly, my horse jerked, twisted, and shied away. The red-bearded guard had done something to her.

As I faced him, the other guard slapped the mare's hind and she shot toward a walled pool. I moved her to the right to miss running headlong into the water, fury igniting my insides.

"You will be sorry!" I shouted over a shoulder as I trotted into the market.

I'd have to find Calev another way. I fisted my hands around the reins. Being nearly an adult was the worst. No one gave you leeway like they did with children. No one gave you respect like they would if I was a year or two older.

Nearby, a merchant called out, selling painted shoes. She had a nice smile so I slid off my horse and approached her. "May I ask you a question?"

She nodded and picked up another pair of shoes to show me. Yellow phoenixes flew over the toes.

"I'm sorry. I don't have coin for new shoes, but I wondered if you could tell me where most of the inns are here?" Maybe Calev had stopped to rest on his way to the kyros.

She shrugged and held out a palm. "Maybe. For two smalls."

Two smalls wasn't much, but it would cost me a meal. "Never mind."

I turned to mount, but a hand on my arm stopped me.

A boy about my age looked down at me. He had nice, dark eyes and his lips lifted at one corner. "The inns are on that side of the city."

As the woman—maybe his mother?—left us to talk, the boy's gaze wandered over my face and clothing. Not many here wore a simple, short shirt and long skirt like I did. I guessed I wore a Pass sort of style, suited to ranging around a boat and dealing with sails.

"But be careful." His tongue danced inside his mouth and made his words sound really beautiful. "Some are not good places for a pretty girl."

Warmth rose along my neck. "Thank you for telling me." I tried to pronounce everything slowly so he'd understand.

A wide smile flashed over his mouth. It was a nice smile. "You don't have to talk like that. I'm fluent in the trade tongue. Despite the accent of my birth language."

I swallowed. "I didn't mean to insult you."

"You didn't. We see many, many visitors here in Akhayma."

Part of me wanted to stay to hear stories about these visitors and his run-ins with them. But most of me pushed to leave, to get to Calev, to help my sister. There really wasn't any sun to spare.

"Thank you," I said. He gave me a quick bow and his jet-black hair shifted over his forehead. "I wish I could stay and talk to you." My cheeks were probably going the color of my poppy-red sash. "But there's an emergency, and I must go."

"Of course." He looked back at his table and tent where stacks of tattered books, small leather pouches, and lengths of rough wool vied for space. "I could come with you?" His eyes widened, hopeful.

My heart beat twice in a breath. "Oh. Yes. That would be… good." It wasn't only because I wanted to hear his voice some more or watch his half smile appear again. It was because he knew the way. This would be faster. Smarter.

∽

We walked Calev's mare through the tangled roads.

"Are we really getting anywhere? It doesn't feel like it. Don't take me through the scenery." I gave him a pointed look. "I don't have the sun for that."

"I wouldn't dream of wasting your day…what is your name?"

"Avigail Raza. Avi. Avi, for short. You can call me Avi." I rolled my eyes at myself.

"I am Radi." He placed a hand on his chest. His fingers were a bit knobby and a strong vein lined his skin, showing he worked hard like I did. "Please call me Radi."

"I'm looking for a friend. My sister's Intended. Do you use that term here?" It was an Old Farm word and I had no idea how to translate it.

"No, but I think I know what you mean." He eased around two men arguing next to a goat freed from its pen. "The one she will marry? Yes?"

I nodded and took a deep breath. The air smelled like animals, tangy spices, and clean water. "His father is the chairman of Old Farm, the native community next to Jakobden, and he has a renewed agreement between Old Farm and Amir Ekrem. He has to get the kyros's sigil applied to it for the agreement to be official. To keep peace in Jakobden."

Radi's eyebrows lifted. "That is important. But you said emergency. What turns this job into something dire? And how are you involved? And please, if you don't care for my questions, feel free not to reply."

The mare tripped on the edge of a stationary cart of rolled rugs, and I urged her left, her feet thudding on the sandy ground.

"I'm only a very curious person," Radi said. "My father says I got it from him."

The thought of family pierced my determination like the tip of a knife to thin skin. "My sister is like that. And our mother was too."

I gripped the reins between thumb and forefinger and set my palm against the mare's neck to feel her familiar coat. I hated being so far from my family, from Kinneret when she was so sick.

"I can tell you. It's nothing that needs to be secret. My sister..." The words didn't want to crawl up my throat. I grabbed each one and threw it out of my mouth. Sweat gathered on my upper lip. "She has a deadly fever."

Radi's black eyes fluttered close for a moment and he briefly touched my hand. His skin was very smooth. "May the Holy Fire help her."

With my thumb, I made the Holy Fire circle on my forehead. "If I can urge her Intended to hurry up with his duty and get home, I think he can save her."

"How?" he asked, hurrying more now.

I liked that my story had prompted him to pick up speed. Around carts of date palms and green vegetables, people with reed baskets on their heads, and well-dressed men and women, we zigzagged through the crowded streets like fish with the current at our backs.

"It's hard to explain," I said. "They need one another. It's like my mother and father were. If Calev comes home, if he is there for her," I tried to swallow around my tight throat, "I really think she'll heal. She's so sick, I..."

Tears rolled out before I could stop them. I sucked my trembling, lower lip into my mouth, knowing I looked like an out-of-control child but unable to stop.

Radi paused and faced me. My pulse ticked more quickly. Fear for Kinneret dwarfed the fact that this fine-faced stranger was being so kind. The crowd streamed around us, bumping gently. A dubious thought wriggled into my head. Why was he helping me so much?

"I'll do what I can," he said. "We'll find the inn and all will be well."

I wanted so much to believe him. I pushed him and nodded to move on. "Talk while we walk. Why *are* you doing this?"

Radi bit his lip, and his throat moved in a swallow as we

rounded a group of women holding one large jug each. "Two reasons." His chest moved with a rough breath. "One. I wanted to leave my family's stall before my cousin came."

"Why?"

"He likes to fight."

"You don't? Or are you not good at it? Or both?" We rounded a corner and split to the right.

"I thought you said your sister was the curious one."

"This isn't curiosity. This is *being aware*."

He grinned. "Ah. I'm very good at fighting. I'm quick."

He flashed a look that was both fierce and dangerous. An odd feeling stirred around my heart. When he turned his head, I wished he'd look at me like that again.

"But I'm not very good at fighting with someone I don't really want to hurt," he said. "I tend to respond with the most vicious attack. My father taught us both. To be safe in the city at night. But my cousin is good at pulling punches and holding back. I get excited and end up hurting him every time."

"It must not be too bad if he comes back for more."

"I still don't like hurting him." Radi frowned.

"And your second reason for helping me?"

"You're rather pretty."

I held my breath, suddenly afraid of doing something to ruin those wonderful words.

"And smart," he said. Well, those words were even better.

Forcing myself to breathe and quit acting like what he said mattered, I tugged the horse to move faster and said, "Fine." I had no idea what else to say.

"Yes. Fine." There was a little laugh in his tone and I wasn't sure I liked that. No, I couldn't lie to myself. I did. I liked it too much.

The water in the canals rushed by the side of the road, protected by small walls marked with painted calligraphy. "Do those words say what section of the city we're in?"

"No. That's the name of the kyros. *Kyros Meric, the Eternally Victorious.* And there and there spell out the name of his wife. *Seren, Pearl of the Desert.*"

"Are we getting any closer?" This was taking too long. Calev would have had to get to the kyros today, finish his duty, and get home. Or just go home and come back later to see the kyros.

"We're here."

Around a bend, a row of tents showed similar wooden signs painted in white pictures and letters, hanging from high posts above the doors.

"Here are the inns. Most of them anyway. See that one?" His first two fingers sent my gaze to a sign with a flower. Wide, open petals hovered above a bunch of words I couldn't read. "That is the Lotus Inn. A nice establishment."

The next one showed a ship and a cupped hand. "And…the Harbor Inn, maybe?"

"Yes. That's it exactly," Radi said. "We can speak to the innkeepers together if you like."

Gratitude loosened my choking grip on the reins. "Please." Who knew if they'd speak the trade tongue? I didn't know a lick of the desert language.

I described Calev to Radi and he did the same, in the desert tongue, to four different innkeepers.

None had seen him.

Radi jerked his chin at the fifth inn's sign. "The Egret's Regret."

Ignoring the name and Radi's wince at the worn-down look

of the place, I rushed to the woman at the front door. "Please. I'm looking for a man. In a headtie." I tried to repeat the phrases Radi had used.

The woman's brow wrinkled.

"We are looking for an Old Farm man with a blue headtie and a handsome face," Radi said. He said some more that I couldn't untangle.

The woman's mouth popped open, and she let out a stream of sounds that overwhelmed me.

Radi nodded then spoke again.

I gripped his sleeve. "Well?"

"She saw him. He was here. Paid to stay last night," he said. "Played cards. Had too much gray plant. Left and never returned."

The air went cold. "No."

"I'm afraid so."

I hefted myself onto the mare's back and held out a hand so Radi could mount up behind me. He was basically a stranger, but I thought I might need him later. Plus, he said nice things. And in a time like this, I needed some nice things.

"He wouldn't have gone far," I said.

The tents butted up to one another for the most part, but a few left alleys between. Flies buzzed over a pile of something smelly in the nearest one. The next held two men slumped against a lotus tower's base. Neither had Calev's hair or silhouette.

"This isn't a lovely part of the city," Radi mumbled beside my ear.

"I noticed."

"If he fell asleep out here, at night…"

"There are bad places in Jakobden too. I used to live in one. You don't have to tell me the risks. I know them. I lived them."

"How old are you?"

"Fifteen and a little more."

"You act older."

"Being poor makes you grow up sometimes." I didn't want to talk about what I'd been through. I had enough on my mind.

Radi squeezed my shoulder gently. "You're well-dressed now. How did that happen?"

"That's a long story. Keep looking for Calev. Please."

"Of course."

If I didn't find him, Kinneret would die like the others in town had. Her fever had come on so fast. Just like Mother and Father's had. I could feel the truth of it like burning metal inside me, like an arrowhead lodged and searing under my ribs.

5
CALEV

An aching pain groaned from more parts than I cared to count. Putting hands on the sandy dirt, I sat up and my head boomed like a tiny cannon had fired between my ears.

"Ugh." I wiped my hand down my face. Dry flakes of blood came off my mouth. My tongue found the split in my lip.

"Old Farm," a voice over me said.

The sun shot over the tents and made it impossible to see who was talking. I held up a hand to shield my eyes. Dark kaftan. Delicate nose.

"What are you doing?" It was the woman who owned the inn. She helped me up and touched my cheek gently, though it still hurt. "Got yourself robbed, eh?"

"I suppose so." Then a shiver rushed through my throbbing head. The agreement.

"What is it? You're alive. It could've been worse."

"No. Not that." I palmed my waist, where my sash used to be. "They stole the parchment. The agreement. It's gone."

She ran a hand down my chest and her mouth tucked up at one side. "You probably lost your money too. I can help you. You can work for me for a few days. Make back what you owe. Get more to travel home?"

I shook my head and untangled her fingers from my tunic. "I have an appointment with the kyros today. He has to apply his sigil to the agreement…the peace might not hold and my father and Amir Ekrem will have to calm the advisors and…"

The cannon in my head blasted more pain that echoed through my scalp. I rubbed at my head, then saw that my smallest finger was bare. They'd taken my sigil ring. My throat went drier than it'd already been.

"They'll never know I'm who I say I am. They'll never know."

"You're Old Farm. Someone in a place of power? You talk of an amir and the kyros."

"My father is Old Farm's chairman. I was sent here to show the kyros the agreement of peace and trade between the Empire and my people. To gain his approval. And his signature. His sigil."

"I know very well what a sigil is," she said quietly, more to herself. One hand hitched onto her hip. She clicked her tongue. "What to do. What to do."

I rammed my fingers through my hair. My headtie was gone too. Those men had stolen everything of value after knocking me out. Without a headtie or an Old Farm sigil ring, the kyros would never believe I was who I was.

"I need to wash. I have to at least try to meet with the kyros."

"Let Samira handle it." She set a finger against her chest. "I know what to do." She hooked her arm through mine.

"Wait. Did you put gray plant on my food? Those men were laughing about it. My head…"

"I did no such thing." She was clearly insulted.

"Fine. But you did tell me stealing didn't happen around here. The whole thing about losing a hand and all that?"

"That's what I tell nervous customers."

"Nice."

Her shrug said it all. "You wandered into the night with an entire stalk of gray plant in your belly."

"They put it on my food. When you weren't looking or something. I didn't—"

"If you'd listened to me last night, Old Farm, you'd be happy and on your way now."

"You didn't tell me anything, Samira."

"I did. You just don't remember."

I took a heavy breath. She was probably right.

What was I going to do? I had no coin, no sigil ring to prove my blood, no parchment to show the kyros. My clothes were ripped in places and a string of blackened blood ran down the front from where my lip had opened up. I was in no condition to present myself to the ruler of most of the known world. A man who, if the stories were true, had a touch of madness that gave his immature nature a jagged edge. I couldn't enter his court looking like a desperate, lying beggar with rocks at the bottom of his grain sack.

Samira led me into the dark glow of the tented inn where she closeted me into a back room with a bowl of clean water and a cloth. She wiped my fingers clean, and because of the world being blurry still and the pain pulsing over my body, I let her finish every knuckle and nail. After a large cup of water soothed my parched throat, the world cleared a little.

"I can clean myself up."

She raised an eyebrow. "You look ready to vomit. Let me help you." The cloth was soft on my cheek and she dragged it down my neck, a new attentive gleam rising in her eyes.

Taking her hand gently—thinking of Kinneret's fierce laugh, the one that squeezed my heart and lifted it—I moved Samira's fingers away. "I can do it. Thank you for all your help."

Pursing her lips, she cocked her head. "All right then. But if you change your mind, handsome and desperate lord, you call out. I'll be at the front." Her hips swayed as she moved toward the door's flap. "Oh wait. I should maybe call you *servant*, eh? You'll need to pay me eventually."

She was enjoying this far too much. And I had the uneasy feeling she was keeping something from me. "Samira, if you think you can force me into a tumble…"

"No, no, lord servant. I'm no criminal. It's a simple matter of working off your time in this room and the food I'm about to give you. Simple business. You'll owe me. Whether or not we tumble." She winked and glided out of the room.

A grumble rose to my lips, but I closed it off. She was right. Father had taught me enough about business outside of Old Farm. Cities like this, even a smaller town like Jakobden, didn't function like my home and my people, giving and taking as needed. *They aren't family,* he'd said. *Only true family can give up food for one another when times are lean.*

Blood came off my chin easily with the wet cloth. Not so from my clothing. I washed my dusty feet. My right shoulder pinched as I stripped my tunic off over my head and I swallowed a squeak of pain. Taking up the needle and thread Samira had left beside the bowl, I turned my tunic inside out and began stitching the two rips along the sides.

I was such a complete and utter fool. I'd be lucky if Kinneret would even look at me after all this, let alone marry me. I'd be lucky if Amir Ekrem didn't take my head. He wouldn't want to, but Serhat would. She'd press him. In the years I'd known her, I'd only seen her not get her way twice.

Samira returned with a steaming plate of flatbread and some sauced vegetable I didn't recognize. I reached for the cup of watered wine she held, but she jerked it away.

"Eat first."

The vegetable tasted green and fresh, the sauce spicy and cinnamon-like. As I drained the weak wine, I realized why Samira had insisted I finish my meal first. The simple bed in the corner blurred. My knees trembled, and I braced myself on the lotus tower that held the establishment upright. Samira's hands felt prickly as she helped me to lie down.

"Sleep, lord servant. You need it."

"What did you…you gave me something…I have to leave now. Can't wait." I tried to argue, but darkness wrapped me up and stole my mind. I'd been drugged. Again.

Fevered dreams bit into my sleep.

In my nightmare, my father and the elders glared at my empty, open hands. Sweat soaked my tunic and blood ran from my lip. Kinneret pushed a curl away from her face and refused to look me in the eye. Explanations sifted from my mouth like useless chaff.

I had to wake up.

Wake up.

But I couldn't. My eyelids wouldn't open.

Can't.

Darkness swamped me.

~

AN ANIMAL'S bray shook me out of my stupor. There was some commotion in the street beyond the inn's thick, woven walls. I had to clear my head. Water. Water will clear the drug away.

The room was nearly black with only a strip of light coming in between the cut in the door's flap. Nearby, someone was humming. My head pounded.

The water, I reminded myself. On the table.

I pushed off the bed and my knees hit the floor. How had that happened? I lowered onto my elbows and pressed my forehead into the thin rug, desperate to ease the throbbing. Fighting a rush of clinging heat and nauseating dizziness, I eased myself to standing and put a hand against my stomach.

Where was my tunic? I only had my small clothes on. Had the woman undressed me? How long had I been out?

The table rocked under my palm and water lipped over the edge of the bowl. I plunged the cup into the cool liquid and drank all I could before I thought my stomach would burst.

Maybe Samira meant to keep me here for some strange purpose. Maybe she just thought she was being helpful. Regardless, I had to leave and I had to leave now.

6
AVI

The street beside the row of inns bustled with men who seemed to be late for important things. Two donkeys and a camel, loaded up with sacks and bedrolls, brayed their opinion on being tied together.

Radi and I had talked to someone at every inn—the owner at all but one whose employee said she was out on an errand. Worry pinched clawed fingers into my shoulders and neck and I couldn't believe it was this hard to find a person. Radi, arms crossed and leaning against a lotus tower's white stone, tapped an elbow, thinking.

"You probably need to get back to your parents' stall in the market," I said.

He yawned wide despite his obvious effort to fight it. His white teeth were straight except for one tooth on top, on the side. "I do. But what's your next idea for finding your brother-in-law to be? I hate to just leave you."

I'd had no luck at the Kyros Walls, but it was really the only place to go. Nothing else stuck out in my mind. "I'll try to get past the kyros's front guards and try to see the kyros himself, or maybe a representative."

Radi held out a hand to lead me back through the maze of tents and people of all colors speaking in three different languages. I took it and gave him the best smile I had in me. I could've figured out a way back on my own. I really just liked the feel of his fingers on mine.

I felt strangely lonely.

I'd only been gone four days, but it felt like so much longer. It was silly. But the foreign tents, languages, and scents were waves crashing over my head. I couldn't seem to get a good breath.

At the market, merchants had set out their tables in front of tents that appeared to serve as both home and goods storage. Beside Radi's family's stall, a woman and a man in rich black clothing haggled with a short man. Their hands moved nearly as fast as their lips.

"Radi!" A young man—a little older than Radi and me—burst from behind the table and knocked a roll of blue wool to the ground. He hugged Radi. "Where've you been? I wanted to try the sweep Nuh showed me.

"That fighter has more patience than my wonderful mother," Radi said. "Are you paying him or something?"

The man I guessed was his cousin laughed and punched Radi in the arm, well, tried to punch him. Radi slipped his shoulder back and the cousin missed.

"No, cousin. He said I remind him of the brother he lost during the Invader attack. Before you were born."

Radi spun and held a hand out toward me. "Bash, this is Avi. She's looking for her brother-in-law. He's needed back at home. They're from Jakobden."

Bash's eyes went wide. "Ooo. Near the Pass. Have you seen a Salt Wraith?"

"I have. It's not something to be happy and excited about."

"Of course. Sorry."

"It's all right. I guess if I hadn't had seen them myself, I might think they're interesting too."

"Her sister is sick," Radi said, "and needs her husband-to-be."

I ran a hand down Arrow's warm nose and let her lip my palm, savoring the feel of her soft horsey lips. "Kinneret has a deadly fever and—"

"Wait." Bash put out a hand. "Your sister is the great Kinneret Raza? Mistress of the Pass?"

"Mistress of the what?"

"The Pass! The one who did all the amazing things that the traders are all talking about." He put his clasped hands over his heart and blinked. "Kinneret Raza."

"Um. Yes. She is. Is everyone really talking about her?" I turned to Radi, who shrugged.

Bash waved Radi off. "Don't ask him. He doesn't talk to anyone who knows anything."

"Except that he happened to spend all morning with Kinneret Raza's sister." I couldn't help but smirk.

"Except for that, yes." Bash smiled. "Why are you here? Oh wait. You said she had a fever?"

Radi cleared his throat. "If you'd shut up for a minute, she could tell you."

I did.

"But," Bash stammered, "but why can't she heal herself? She's amazing!"

"She's not a healer. My aunt is. She's on her way from Kurakia, but I don't know if she'll get to Jakobden in time."

"Aren't there other healers?"

"Yes. And the amir has called them in. No one has been able to heal her. A lot of people have this fever." I turned to Radi. "Thank you, for all you've done to help. I need to go now."

"I'll be here if you need a place to stay tonight."

"I'll find him today. I have to. I have to get back home."

He nodded, and his cousin smiled sadly. I left them explaining everything to Radi's parents, who were curious about where he'd been all morning. Radi gave me one last look and I tried to memorize his features. I didn't want to forget the boy who'd been so kind to me or the way his fingers had felt on mine.

∼

"YOU CANNOT PASS," the guards at the Kyros Walls said. "Public supplications take place tomorrow. Today is only for those with appointments to see the kyros or his retinue."

"I just need to see if my brother-in-law is here. He does have an appointment with the kyros, for the amir in Jakobden." I wasn't sure exactly how that worked, but I wasn't going to tell this guard. "He's probably inside, waiting for a meeting right now." Since he hadn't been at any of the inns, this was the only answer.

"Right."

"Why don't you believe me? Do you really hear stories like

this all the time? This is because I'm not from Akhayma." I looked to the skies as another group of people—blessed appointment holders, I had to assume—sidled past me and walked happy as you please into the kyros's courtyard.

"No," the first guard said. "We have many visitors."

"Then it's my age. I'm a little girl so you can't let me in to see the big important kyros."

"Say it again, and you become our prisoner. No one is to speak ill of the kyros." He eyed the five bells on my sash. "Even if you are high-caste. You can wait until the supplicant's day."

"When is that again?" My mind was flying from one idea to another, all of them worthless.

"Tomorrow."

"I can't wait. This is important." My vision blurred, and I wiped my hand across my eyelashes. "Please. Isn't there someone else I can ask?" Kinneret could be dying right now. Or what if I waited one night, then she died on our way home? "There has to be a system for this sort of thing, for emergencies, right? Help me, please." I palmed my eyes again, angry that I couldn't seem to stop crying.

"That's enough," the second guard said.

A man in a rippling black kaftan and a well-dressed party rode up to the gates, blocking my view. I swallowed and nudged my horse away from the entrance, veering left and following a stream of men and women with steel at their belts and shiny, pointed helmets. I pounded a fist against the saddle in front of me. Arrow snorted.

"Sorry." I sighed. I was apologizing to a horse. I needed some sleep.

As I let Arrow stop to snuffle a patch of green near the canals, a skinny little boy with wild hair threw a stick into the air. My thoughts shifted and surfaced, one by one, in my head. None of my ideas would work. I couldn't pretend to have an appointment now. The guards had seen me. I didn't have enough money with me to bribe someone with an appointment to bring me in with them. Everyone gaining entrance had looked like clan chieftains anyway. They weren't going to care about one kaptan in a faraway township. My gaze followed the spin of the boy's stick as he tossed it up again.

I had to think like Kinneret. She never let anything get in the way of what she wanted.

The little boy caught the stick neatly between his teeth. Amazing. Especially considering flames flickered at the ends of the stick. A crowd gathered around him, stomping their feet in praise and tossing him small coins. A girl and a boy, siblings from the look of their similar noses, ran past.

"I'm going to tell Mother about that new boy!" the girl said.

Her brother nodded. "Su will want to see too. I'll get him."

I searched the crowd for Calev. "Calev ben Y'hoshua! Where are you?"

The noise of merchants calling out, hooves on the ground, and the rush of everyday life in this big city trampled my shouts.

If only I could toss fire and catch it in my mouth. Then maybe I could get everyone's attention. Or at least Calev's.

I huffed a breath. What would Kinneret do?

Wait. That's it. I tugged Arrow to a stop beside a man selling ponies. If I did something that got everyone's attention, surely Calev would find me.

But what could I do?

"You want to sell your fine mount?" The pony merchant set a gentle hand on my horse's neck.

"No. Thank you." I had an idea. A foolish plan. "I think I'm going to need her for a ladder."

This was the stupidest idea I'd ever had. But it was just the sort of thing Kinneret would do and somehow get away with.

"What?" The merchant scratched his head.

I dug my heels into Arrow's sides and drove through the crowded street toward the Kyros Walls, a good length from where the guards stood so if they came after me, I could get back on Arrow and ride away, into the crowd. I edged Arrow sideways against the pale stone, took my feet from the stirrups, and went to a crouch on the saddle. Arrow huffed and side-stepped.

"Easy now. Be still."

Using the balance I'd learned on boats, I stood on her back and reached as high as I could. I needed handholds to climb. Arrow shifted her weight onto one back hoof and I caught myself against the wall, heart drumming.

"Girl, what are you doing?" The pony merchant had followed me. He stood below, taking Arrow's reins.

"Don't worry about it."

"Can I have your horse when you fall and crack your head open?" Seeing my scowl, he let go of the reins. "Such a face on such a young person."

"Mind your own business." I was going to fall and this was so stupid. But I couldn't wait another night to get to Calev. Kinneret was dying. Every minute here was a minute wasted.

He held out his hands. "All right. Don't say I didn't warn you."

Finally, my fingers dug into a space between the stones. I jammed a sandal into another uneven place in the Kyros Walls and pushed, leaving the saddle's surface. My other foot dangled

FEVER

as I shuffled it around and searched for a little ledge, a flaw in the quarried white rock, some mortar that could be crumbled away. Sweat gathered under my shirt. My caste bells jingled as if they worried I was going to fall.

A woman below gasped and said something in the desert tongue. Another voice replied. They were almost right under me.

"Just some...entertainment. For the kyros. That's all. No problem here," I panted, knowing full well I looked completely mad climbing up the wall.

I shifted to another set of handholds. The top of the wall was only an arm's length away. I reached and reached, my one lodged foot shaking, and grasped the high, toothed edge of the walls. A sad grin split my dry lips. Kinneret would've loved to be here doing this with me. Normally, I would've told her to stop being a crazy person. But I had to risk this for her. If I could get Calev's attention, get him home, she'd be all right. I was sure of it. My heart thrummed with the truth of it.

I waved my arms. "Calev ben Y'hoshua!"

The crowd—a clutter of black and red and orange kaftans—teemed on both sides of the walls. A huge black-blue tent with star-shaped panels of silvery material commanded the kyros's courtyard. Smaller tents, with people going in and out, surrounded it. Some paths were lined with smooth rock and a simple stable at the far end revealed swishing animal tails and servants with large bells suspended over their heads and attached to metal belts. A few faces peered up at me. I had to be louder.

"Calev ben Y'hoshua! I'm looking for Calev! An Old Farm with black hair and an agreement from Jakobden's amir!"

Only a few more people looked up. I was going to have to be

like the boy with the fire stick. I tied my skirt between my legs so I wouldn't give *that* kind of show, placed my hands on the wide surface of the top of the wall, and lifted myself into a handstand.

"Avi!" Radi's voice bounced up to me.

My elbow buckled.

Someone else shouted.

I caught myself. My lungs were about to burst.

"Avi, you have to get down! You'll be arrested!" Radi's words were strained, high-pitched in his stress.

"Is everyone paying attention?"

"Yes, for Holy Fire's sake, yes. Get down! I have a cousin— very, very distant but still— who works for the kyros's wife. Her name is Meekra. Mother said she thinks she is her handmaiden. Mother said we might be able to get a message to her and some information if we're lucky. Get down, please!"

I lowered my feet and stood upright, looking not at Radi's side of the wall, but toward the courtyard. High castes and nobles stared, their servants gawking beside them.

"If you meet a Calev ben Y'hoshua," I called out, cupping my hand to my mouth, "tell him to find his sister at…" I couldn't name somewhere everyone knew in case the guards decided to come after me. "…at the place he would feel most comfortable!" I repeated the message, then noticed a shift in the crowd by the gates. I spun to see the guards, on the other side of the wall, pushing through the people and toward Radi.

"Run!" I called to him.

"No! I'll help you down. Start climbing. I'll help you!"

"Just go!" The guards were already closing in. "Go!"

Radi positioned Arrow below me. "Hurry!"

My thundering pulse choked me. I rubbed my palms on my skirt, untied the knot, and lowered myself onto my stomach. I found a foothold and pretty soon Radi's guiding whispers were nearer. With my feet on the saddle again, I took Radi's hand.

"Come on!" I jerked on his fingers to get him to jump up onto Arrow behind me.

He huffed, then mounted easily, his muscled calf showing as his kaftan billowed.

"Go!" I shouted into Arrow's ear. She lurched forward. We were going to get away.

Large hands thrust through the crowd and grabbed the reins, jerking us to a stop.

Radi and I slid from Arrow's back. The ground jarred my body and my teeth banged together.

The first guard clamped down on my wrist and hefted me up. "Don't even believe you are high-caste."

"This one definitely isn't," the second guard said.

Radi set his jaw as the man put a yatagan's long, steel edge to his throat.

My skin felt too thin and my heart beat in my ears. "Please. You must let me speak to the kyros. Or his advisor. I'm not lying."

The guards led us—along with Arrow who certainly didn't deserve to be a part of all this—to the back of the city.

"This boy's cousin is the kyros's handmaiden. We need to speak to her. Where are you taking us?" I asked. "To see the kyros?"

The guards laughed and Radi shook his head. "They're taking us to the cells."

My bones were hollow. My heartbeat echoed through them.

"Radi. I'm so sorry. You should've run. I'm so, so sorry."

"You didn't force me to do anything. I'm here because I want to be. Well, I don't want to be here exactly. But, you know."

"Shut your mouths," the first guard spat as we crossed under a huge arch and into a sloped area filled with archery targets, a long row of what looked like stables, low buildings crowded with armed fighters, and a line of barred cells. The sun burned the image into my eyes and a shiver tugged at my limbs.

They were going to cage us like animals.

A stable boy ran up, and with direction from the guards, took Arrow to the stables. As her shiny coat and silky tail disappeared, my stomach worked its way toward my throat. She was my only way home. I couldn't make it back to Jakobden on foot. Not on my own.

The guards pushed Radi and me into the same cell.

"Wait, please," Radi said. "My cousin Meekra works for Pearl of the Desert. Can you at least send a message to her? She won't know my name but—"

The guard ignored Radi.

The clang of the bolt sliding shut blasted through me, turning my legs to pudding. I curled a hand around the bars to keep from falling.

Radi winced, his face a mask of pity. Two men and a woman crouched in the back corners, their clothing in rags and their faces thin. They looked at us like we might eat them for breakfast.

"Avi." Radi grasped the bars and looked into the training field. "What are we going to do now?"

I dropped to my knees and stared at the lock, with no idea how to escape. We were trapped. Maybe for the rest of our lives. Worrying for Kinneret, I'd acted like her. Reckless. Not at all like myself. I should have planned and taken my time. Figured out something smart instead of climbing walls like a fool. And now Kinneret was going to die without Calev to save her and without her only family at her side.

I put my head in my hands and cried.

7
CALEV

My stomach growled as I dried my hands on the cloth near a pile of clean platters. I'd spent an entire day, a night, and most of this day too working off what I owed Samira, picking up after idiots who acted like I had my first night here. Now I had to leave. To get to the kyros.

Today was an open supplication day for people who didn't have formal appointments, messages from foreign rulers or any of the Empire's amirs. Today, even as a ragged nobody, I could get into the Kyros Walls. What I would do once I had the kyros's attention, I wasn't sure, but the sun hung low in the sky and there was no time left for wondering. The last rays pierced the tent and gave Samira's inn the glow of blood.

"Leaving so soon?" Checking that none of the patrons peered over her countertop, Samira set two bags of coin in a hole under a wooden carving of a desert lion.

"Yes. You said the kyros sees anyone today, right?"

She nodded. "And in five days, he will again."

"In five days, I'll be at home."

"What are you going to show the kyros to prove your story?"

"He'll believe me."

The slant of her eyebrow told me she didn't think so, but I didn't care. I had to try.

"Thank you for all the help. I won't forget what you did for me."

Samira's eyebrow lifted mockingly. "Ah, it was nothing. If you want to work again tonight and get a meal out of it, come back to me, lord servant."

"*Lord servant* isn't a title I relish. I think my time wearing it is over."

"So haughty is the lord servant! We'll see how you feel when the kyros throws you out on your handsome bum."

"Goodbye, Samira."

"May the Holy Fire bless you."

"But not so much that I won't work out an indenture to you for the rest of my days, hm?"

She smiled wide. "That's about right."

THE LINE GOING through the Kyros Walls snaked around the oasis pool and through the market. It was nearly nightfall, and I was close enough to study the hilt of a guard's yatagan. Small pomegranates decorated the length of it and made me miss home.

Or did I?

Father was going to explode when he heard all of this. He'd

publicly punish me at best and Kinneret would never have me as her husband. At worst, I'd be cast out of Old Farm.

My empty stomach rolled.

Father and the amir were expecting me by nightfall in two days. My failure would shame Ekrem as the new amir. The agreement between the Empire—with Jakobden's amir as representative—and Old Farm had been continuous and peaceful for two hundred years.

My knuckles pressed into my forehead where my headtie had been until the robbery.

Had I already started problems between the people at home? Had I already lost my people's chance to remain as we were, with our own traditions and commerce, separate from the Empire?

Surely, Amir Ekrem would be merciful. He was a good man. But even if he and his advisors didn't begin tougher negotiations or accuse Old Farm of not taking his rule seriously, I would still be seen as a failure and a fool. How would I provide for Kinneret without my position?

I blew out a breath, staring at the people in front of me. Why was this taking so long?

I nudged the man in front of me. "Sorry, but do you think we'll get in today?"

The man bunched his lips. "Hmm. Maybe?" He shrugged and crossed his arms in a strange way with both hands on top of his forearms.

Closing my eyes, I prayed very, very hard.

"You," a deep voice said.

It was a new man. He wore a warrior's kaftan and pants, but with detailed embroidery around the collar and down the sleeves. He had a bright blue sash devoid of bells, which spoke of his pure desert bloodline. His gaze went from my own clothing to my face like he was looking for clues.

"Come. Why are you here?" he asked.

Hope soared inside my chest. Hope mixed with the fear of falling into even worse trouble. Following him through the Kyros Walls, I explained everything. By the time I stopped talking, we'd arrived at the finest tent, the one with stars along its top.

"I don't believe this wild story." The man didn't look at me as he said those terrible words. Instead, he peered inside the kyros's tent and pulled something green from his sash. "But I do know the kyros was set to meet with an Old Farm representative. Yesterday."

So even if I did gain entrance and did everything right, I'd still be on his bad side for missing the appointment. My stomach rolled. Kyros Meric was known to be mercurial. One wrong word and your life was forfeit. I swallowed. I had to keep my wits about me and do the best I could.

"It's the truth," I said to the warrior. "I swear it. Ask me anything about Old Farm."

"There have been strange tales coming out of Jakobden. No one quite understands what happened to dispose Amir Mamluk. And the talk about that girl and her abilities with the cursed waters there…"

"Kinneret. She is my Intended."

"Your Intended?"

"She will be my wife."

"And tomorrow you'll be the kyros, yes?"

"No. I'm serious. I was with her during the discovery of hidden Ayarazi. The deaths…the—"

"Enough. Your story is interesting. The kyros won't want to

hear all of it, but his wife, Seren, Pearl of the Desert, will. And I, Erol, one of her personal guards, do everything I can to please her."

His black eyes shone as he guided me into the tent and pressed the green something from his sash into my hand. "Chew this mint so you'll be presentable to the royals."

I did as I was told, thinking of what Oron would say. He would've made some comment now about better places to stick that mint. I wished I could laugh.

My guide Erol walked over to the copper Holy Fire bowl and passed a hand over the flames, praying silently. He gave me a look. Though I wasn't wearing my sigil ring or my Old Farm headtie, I had to show them I was who I said I was.

I shook my head, politely refraining from worshipping like the rest of the Empire. The guide's eyebrows rose, but he dipped his chin in acknowledgment and led me up a long rug where I bowed to the royal couple and their general.

The kyros leaned on the arm of his silver gilt chair, looking bored. His wife, Seren, Pearl of the Desert, stood tall in a dark blue kaftan, a yellow sash and—like the old amir had in Jakobden—she wore a slim length of leather around her head. A single, high-caste bell hung from the tie, touching a spot between the eyebrows.

After the guide spoke to them, Seren smiled kindly, but her eyes were tired. Being a kyros's wife probably wasn't the easiest of roles and she'd only been married a few weeks. Despite the tired eyes, she looked as young as Kinneret.

The kyros himself was a weasel of a man. Just the way he sat, angled away from his wife and with that sulky posture told me everything I needed to know.

He looked me up and down. "You claim to be Amir Ekrem and Chairman Y'hoshua ben Aharon's emissary?"

"Yes, my kyros." My words shook a little, but I managed not to sound like the idiot I was.

"Where is the agreement? Am I to apply my symbol, my royal sigil, to your forehead?"

Some of the courtiers around laughed, but most narrowed their eyes like I'm sure I did. His wife, Seren, breathed out through her nose, irritated.

"It would be an honor, my kyros, but I doubt the ink would hold under the weight of three days of hot travel."

Kyros Meric smiled. "Perhaps you're right. Can you tell the details of the agreement?"

He'd need them to create a new copy to sign and seal. He also probably wanted them so he could check my story.

"Of course, my kyros."

As I started detailing the bushels of lemons and olives and the amount of barley and wheat we'd produced on average the last ten years, my tongue moved slowly and my mind whirred facts out too quickly. I stumbled over percentages of profit through trade.

Erol said something quietly in the desert tongue. The kyros nodded and shifted in his chair.

I smoothed my wrinkled, sashless tunic and tried not to worry about what he'd said. "So the amir will keep thirty percent of the late harvest trade profit and an eighth of the actual products."

The kyros waved impatiently. "Fine. Fine. But what happened to you? Why are you presenting yourself to me like a pauper?"

"I was robbed, my kyros."

He sat up, a hand on the hilt of his personal dagger. An emerald winked at me. "In my city? No."

"Yes."

Every sound in the room blinked out of existence.

All I could hear was my own heart beating the consequence of what I'd done. I'd publicly disagreed with Kyros Meric. My life was forfeit.

Pressing my lips together, I bowed low, pressing my forehead into the rug. My heart pounded erratically.

Shaking, I lifted my gaze and saw Erol speaking with the kyros. Seren put a hand on Kyros Meric's arm, her eyes imploring.

"You should die for your disrespect," the kyros said.

My stomach clenched. I forced myself to keep breathing. I had so many more things to do in life. I didn't want it to be over yet. I wanted to become chairman of Old Farm, to enjoy my engagement to Kinneret, to be Avi's brother and Oron's confidant.

"But I won't have you killed just yet," he said. "If you are who you say you are…well, I won't put the Old Farm chairman's son to death so quickly." The kyros nodded to two guards. "Take him to the cells. I'll have to think on what to do."

The cells? As in, prison?

I held up my hands. "Perhaps, my kyros, if you sent a rock dove to Old Farm and asked them to verify my story—"

The guards grabbed my arms. Their fingers dug into the bruises from the robbery, but the pain lancing through me had nothing to do with flesh and bone. My pain was the agony of knowing I had failed, miserably, utterly, and totally failed.

I imagined Father's angry eyes, the dejected set to his mouth when he learned his eldest son was rotting in a cell in Akhayma.

In my mind, I saw confusion twist Kinneret's beautiful face and could almost hear her arguing that the story couldn't be true, that her Calev wouldn't do something so stupid, that I'd never risk staying at a low inn or fall to thieves during such an important mission.

Before I closed my eyes and let the guards drag me from the tent, I saw Seren whispering in Kyros Meric's ear. Probably yet another person shocked at my behavior, at my lack of propriety, at what they believed were lies.

As they walked me to a row of barred rooms near the military training facilities, I hated myself more and more. Because I'd been in a hurry to rest and eat, I'd spend my life wasting away in the kyros's prison.

8
AVI

Radi elbowed me and jerked his chin toward the other cells. "A new prisoner."

"We have to focus on how we can get out of here."

The man they threw into a cell two down from ours had shoulder-length black hair. I squinted. Something about him plucked a string in me.

I hurried to the far side of the cell and looked again. Dirty tunic. Definitely not from here. From Jakobden. But the fabric. The little red spots—

"Pomegranates!"

The noise of the training field—yatagans banging together and horses galloping—covered my outburst.

Radi eyed me like I'd gone as mad as the man humming in the corner. I grabbed the front of Radi's kaftan and shook him.

"That's my brother-in-law!"

I pushed away from him to go see again, to make sure. It was impossible. But I was almost sure.

Radi came up beside me. "Don't yell to him until those guards leave. You'll draw the wrong kind of attention."

"But that guard is here all the time. What about him?"

"He's a middle-caste guard. He won't care as much as the high-caste ones."

I did notice the bells on the permanent guard's shoulders. But a shout built up behind my lips regardless. I had to call out to Calev, to get him to turn around, to see if it really was him. The high-caste guards traded words with the middle-caste guard, and they grumbled. One made some sort of joke and they all laughed before the high-caste ones stalked away, heading toward the city's back gate.

"Calev!" I hissed. My bones pressed into my skin, into the bars, like I could squeeze through if I only tried hard enough. "It's Avi!"

Radi kept an eye on the guard, who scraped something off the bottom of his boot and spit into the dirt.

The cell between us and the man I thought might be Calev was crowded. Eleven people milled about the space, blocking my view.

"Move!" I waved an arm at them.

One woman glared at me and chewed her thumbnail. Everyone else completely ignored me.

I growled and bumped the bars with the bottom of my fist.

Radi began speaking to the people in the next cell. The foreign words sounded so beautiful, though I didn't have time for beauty right now. Several faces looked up at him. Most shifted to the front of the cell.

The man I hoped was Calev had his arms crossed and his

back to me. His body was coiled with anger, probably frustration.

"Calev!"

He spun. Familiar eyes widened. Inside me, joy opened her arms and threw happy tears down my cheeks.

Calev flung himself against the bars, his face pale. "What are you doing here?" His words were a shaking sail in an undecided wind.

"Me? What are *you* doing here? You should be honored. You're doing the amir's work. And the chairman's. Why did they lock you up?"

Calev's gaze flicked between me and Radi. "Because I'm an idiot."

"I'm going to need more than that." I pressed my forehead against the metal.

As he ran hands through his hair, a purple bruise showed along his forearm. And another under his cheek. His headtie was gone. It was obvious something terrible had happened to him.

I sighed and introduced Radi. "He helped me look for you. The guards here wouldn't let me into the courtyard. When we failed, I climbed the Kyros Walls and went a little mad trying to get everyone's attention, to see if you were around."

Calev bent at the middle, shoulders moving in a heavy breath, then straightened. "I was careless. I stayed at a low-fare inn and drank too much. Let down my guard. Stayed in an inn I shouldn't have. Some men laced my food with gray plant, then robbed me. They took the agreement between Jakobden and Old Farm. They took my ring." He held up a hand, his lips tipped low at the edges.

I scratched my head and blinked.

Calev nodded and looked away.

"You *are* an idiot," I said.

Radi made a noise that said he disagreed.

"Well? He is. How could you, Calev? You have everything. Why would you risk it by being careless in a city you don't know?"

"Says the girl who was arrested for climbing the Kyros Walls," Radi said quietly, raising an eyebrow.

I flashed him a glare.

"There's no excuse," Calev said. "I was careless. Arrogant." He breathed out heavily. "Then I presented myself to the kyros. I told him everything. But he didn't believe I'd been robbed and my mouth moved before I could stop it and I disagreed with him. Out loud."

Radi sucked in a startled breath. A few of the people in the other cell turned their heads to stare at Calev.

"I'm guessing that isn't a good thing," I said.

"No," Radi said. "He should already be dead. I'm surprised he's not. The kyros is…" He eyed the guards and let the words fall into silence.

"I only wanted to assure him that I was telling the truth," Calev said. "I've made a mess of everything I've done since I entered this city. The kyros said he wanted to think about what to do with me."

My news, news of home, thrashed around in my chest like a screaming rabbit ripped open by a fox. I had to tell him. Even though he looked ready to break into a thousand pieces already, shame cracking his features and movements. He needed to know about the fever.

"I came here to get you," I said. "To bring you back fast."

Calev cocked his head, listening.

My throat burned, and my happy tears from earlier began to sting my skin. "Kinneret is dying."

He went still, his hands frozen at his sides. It looked like he'd stopped breathing.

"She has a fever." The truth scraped claws against my heart. "Many have already died from it. It's the same one that killed our parents. But if you go to her, if you're with her, she'll find the strength to heal. She'll fight it and win."

"Did your aunt come over from Kurakia?"

"We sent a rock dove, asking her to come and try to heal Kinneret and the others. But it takes time for word to get across the Pass this time of year."

Nodding, Calev paced a small circle, his hands in his hair again. "She can't heal herself."

I shook my head. "She tried. She's too weak. She keeps thinking she hears Mother and Father. Then she wakes and is crushed by their loss all over again. The fever has her mind." I squeezed the bars until the pain of it stopped my tears.

Calev's gaze snapped to my face. He didn't have to say a word. I knew exactly what his eyes were saying.

We have to get out of here now.

"Enough talk," the guard barked in trade tongue. He knocked the hilt of his dagger on our cell door. "More noise means less food."

The people in the cell between Calev and us shifted apart and Calev disappeared from view.

I breathed out and looked at the ceiling. "Radi. What can we do?" I whispered.

"I don't know. He won't listen to us. None of them will."

We tucked ourselves into the far corner, away from the

humming madman and the guard who walked the strip of dirt in front of the cells.

"If I could get word to my family," Radi said, "maybe my cousin Bash could bribe the guards. Such a slight offense as yours…I don't think they'd come after you. More important worries on their minds. But your brother-in-law, well, his offense is great. I don't know, Avi. I don't know what we could do even if we weren't trapped alongside him." Radi's eyes were serious, burning.

Shaking, I took his hand, held it to my chest. "Thank you for caring. I'm so, so sorry you're here because of me, because of us."

He gripped my fingers and his mouth tried to smile, but only managed a lift on one side. "I made my choices. This isn't your fault. Or your brother's."

He set his forehead against mine and we shared a breath. He was still a stranger, but a stranger I was glad to have on my side.

9
CALEV

The moon hid behind billowing clouds, leaving us prisoners in the gray night. The floor of the cell was nothing but cold dirt, and though all I wanted was to rage my way out of this place and back to Kinneret, exhaustion dragged me into a fevered dream.

We were on Kinneret's boat.

The small dhow dipped in the water and the one triangular sail snapped in a burst of sudden wind. In my dream, the hull was just big enough for us to lie down beside one another.

"What are we going to dream about, Calev?" Kinneret's voice was low and teasing in my ear.

In my mind, her breath flowed over my temple as she pressed the length of her strong legs, stomach, and chest against me.

I shivered.

She smelled like sea salt and the night flowers that lined the path away from town. Her eyes were almost the same light color, contrasting with her dark skin. She thought Miriam's dark eyes were prettier, and maybe they were, but Kinneret was Kinneret. Her coloring meant little. She could've had purple spotted eyes and I'd still think she was perfect. Perfect for me, anyway.

"Tell me," she whispered in my dream.

I decided to show her instead of wasting time talking.

Her lips parted slightly as I kissed her. A warmth stirred deep inside me, and I smiled into her jaw, then the long column of her neck, pulling her closer. She was so soft and had so many angles and curves.

I was lost. I was found.

Still dreaming, my hand drifted over her stomach and my thumb passed over the arch of a rib, the smooth skin. She made a noise, a gentle exhale, and I couldn't stay still. I moved onto my elbows and cradled her beneath me, her head in my hands.

"This could prove an embarrassing kind of dream to have in a prison cell, my love." Her laugh made her body buzz against my hips and chest.

I planted a kiss under her earlobe where her pulse beat, then slid a hand to her lower back, her shirt crumpling under my palm. She wrapped her arms around my neck and tangled her fingers in my hair, grabbing a little roughly. A grin tugged at my lips.

"I don't care," I said into her soft, soft skin.

"Yes, you do."

"No. I really don't." I aligned our bodies and inhaled, my stomach smoothing across hers. "And I think we need less clothing on. Now."

She put hands on my chest, her eyes widening. "Something's wrong."

I sat up. The boat melted away.

Everything in the dream was black except for us.

Kinneret's face paled and she looked at her hands. Her fingers curled into skeletal claws.

She gasped. Or I did.

"What's happening?" I patted her head and came away with strands of her hair. My stomach twisted. "Are you sick?"

When I met her eyes again, her pupils dilated. She fell back. I caught her. Bones pressed through her skin and a scream built inside my throat.

"No!"

The nightmare shattered and I was awake again.

And then I saw the cell door, the rising sun over Akhayma's military training field, and Avi's worried face peering through the bars two cells down from mine.

I turned, kneeled in the corner, and vomited.

"Bring him some water, please!" Avi called out to the guard.

The man grumbled but opened my cell door and handed me a sloshing bowl of cool liquid. Surprised that he cared, I drank a sip, but couldn't manage the rest, instead setting it on the ground. I wiped my mouth with my sleeve and stood on shaking legs, hoping the guard's behavior meant something positive.

Radi and Avi stood staring through the bars.

"You all right?" Radi asked, kindness in his eyes.

I nodded, my skin throwing off the scent of fear and my mind shoving out images of Kinneret's skeletal hands in the dream.

The guard was sharpening his dagger on a whetstone, and the brass studs on his leather vest reflected the Holy Fire in the bowl beside a plate of chicken.

"Do you know my story?" I asked him quietly. I had to get out of here.

He stopped and glanced my way. "Old Farm. Or maybe not." A shrug lifted his shoulders.

"My father is the chairman."

"Rich boy."

"Yes, I am." The words left a bitter taste on my tongue. "And I could make you richer."

"How is that exactly? From what I can tell, you are trapped in a cell and have nothing but the ratty tunic on your *blessed* back."

"For now. But when I leave here—"

"No sign of that happening anytime soon."

Avi and Radi came forward, listening from their cell.

"It could happen right now," I said. "There could be men on their way here to release me, to apologize, to send me on my way to do Old Farm business."

The guard went back to sharpening. I raised my voice, just a little.

"Then you'd be the same. Stuck in this lowly position. Guarding filth. No glory here, hm? Unless you count the redistribution of waste materials." I wiggled my eyebrows at the chamber pot by the door.

Standing, the guard narrowed his eyes. "Do you want to be beaten? Because I can arrange that. Even from my *lowly position*."

"Or," I whispered as he came close, "you could leave my door and that one over there open before you leave and find yourself the lucky recipient of a rich, unnamed uncle's gift in five days when I've had time to return home unscathed and put things in order. No one would need to know if you used the silver wisely, slowly."

I almost sounded like Oron. He would've sworn or made it all seem even dirtier than this bribery attempt really was.

Dagger in hand, the guard rubbed his chin with a knuckle. "It's tempting. We'll see, blessed, rich boy. We'll see."

Every bit of me wanted to beg, to tell my story, to paint a picture of Kinneret and her suffering and try to play on his sympathy. But my time with Oron had taught me that some men had no sympathy. Maybe this stone-faced guard was one of those sad souls. I retreated before I ruined my chance at success.

A new guard jogged up to the older guard. They traded some words and the old guard started toward the city. He looked over his shoulder and pursed his lips, shaking his head a fraction. My heart fell. I held tight to the bars to keep from sliding to the ground. Avi and Radi whispered together, Avi's frown making everything worse.

I'd failed. We were stuck.

The new guard opened Avi's cell and jerked her arm, holding out shackles. Radi stepped forward, but the guard shouldered him back expertly. With Avi in chains, the guard welcomed another guard into the cell and they grabbed Radi, ringing his wrists in metal too.

I slammed a hand on the door as the new guards shackled Radi and Avi.

"Where are you taking them?"

The guards' silence flooded my mind with the nightmare about Kinneret—her hair falling from her head, the grip fear had on her voice.

Avi looked at me with big eyes.

A shudder wrapped around me.

The shorter of the two guards led them away—To their punishments? To their deaths?—and it was as if Kinneret's life drained step by step, heartbeat to heartbeat.

A shout built in my lungs, and I unleashed it, seeing red.

The taller guard kicked the door. "You should behave. I'm to take you to the kyros for your sentencing."

My hands fell to my sides.

Avi and Radi's silhouettes blended into the walls' shadow as the city took them.

I stepped back, trying to keep my frustration in check as the guard opened my door. He linked my hands with thick, steel shackles engraved with the Kyros Meric's title. I was marked as his property. No better than a cow, fit to be used or slain as he saw fit.

THE KYROS WASN'T SITTING at the high table in the main tent this time. Instead his general and his wife Seren regarded supplicants with serious eyes, explaining the kyros wasn't well today.

While a middle-caste woman detailed who she believed had murdered her husband and a high-caste man my age explained a bad trade with one of the steppe's noble clans, my heart jumped from erratic, jolting beats to sluggish rolls that left me dizzy.

Kinneret, I will get back to you. Be strong. Be strong.

Finally, it was my turn.

My knees hit the carpet.

The general's aged voice rumbled through my spinning head. "Stand. Give your name."

Putting a hand on my knee, I managed to straighten. I raised my chin and did my best to give him the look my father would've. "I am Calev ben Y'hoshua, son of Old Farm's chairman, Y'hoshua ben Aharon."

"You spoke out against the kyros, Calev ben Y'hoshua."

"I am sorry, General, and Pearl of the Desert." I knelt again. "It was an accident born of frustration."

Seren waved a hand so I would rise up. "Tell us your story, Calev ben Y'hoshua. Not about the agreement and the robbery. Tell us about your connection to the girl and boy who threatened the kyros's peaceful home with a dangerous and disrespectful stunt on the top of the Kyros Walls."

"Please, will you tell me where they are? Where they've been taken? She is my Intended's sister. The man, the boy, he is a friend of hers. The girl, Avigail, came here to bring me home. My Intended, Kinneret, is dying of a fever."

"The girl and boy are being questioned by the lower bench. As a favor to my new husband. Are you a healer of some sort?"

"No."

"Then this is all a story to waste our time," the general snapped.

"Avi believes that if I go to Kinneret, she'll heal. She'll be able to fight the fever until her aunt, who is a healer, arrives."

"Why?" Seren's look intensified.

"Because we love one another."

The general made a noise and crossed his arms, but Seren's eyes narrowed and she asked me to tell her more.

"I don't know if Avi is right," I said. "I've seen plenty in the last year to let me know there is much in the world that is… difficult to understand. Maybe she's right. Maybe my love for

Kinneret can save her. I'll do anything to try it. It's all I have to give."

"Love is all you have to give," Seren said in a whisper.

I nodded. "Yes, Pearl of the Desert."

The general jerked a hand at some men. "Take him back to the cells."

Seren opened her mouth to say something, but no words came out. Her silence took my breath and made the world seem too heavy to bear. Was she going to save me? I would likely never know.

10
AVI

Rain trampled down from black clouds and onto my head where I stood, back in our cell. I'd thought it hardly ever rained in Akhayma. My heart chilled.

Had Calev's luck run out?

With shaking fingers, I rung out my hair, then braided it again. Radi stared into the training fields, unblinking. I put a hand on his arm, feeling like I'd known him for so much longer than I had.

"What are you thinking?"

"About Meekra. About how we might drive the guards crazy until they decide to send a message."

Leaning against the bars, I searched the cells for Calev. He stood at the front, near the door, his forehead pressed into the metal and rain dripping off his chin and the scant beard growing there.

"Calev."

He didn't move. I eyed the guards, not wanting to push our luck. Some more important looking people had questioned us while Calev spoke to the kyros. They'd frowned and murmured to themselves, then sent us back here. At least we weren't dead yet. I supposed Calev had nothing to share since he'd been silent as stone when we got back, only gasping in relief to see us alive.

"Calev!" His head turned and one hand slid down the bars. "Did you see Pearl of the Desert's handmaiden?"

His eyebrows drew together as Radi came up beside me. I stood closer, enjoying his warmth in the wet, chilly rain.

"Maybe. There were several there serving…"

Radi pushed into the front corner to get closer to Calev. "Was there a girl named Meekra? Or something like that?"

Calev shook his head. "I didn't hear any names. Why?"

"She's my cousin," Radi said. "Distant cousin. I don't think she knows. I thought maybe if she was told we were related, maybe Pearl of the Desert would be more apt to listen to our story."

The man at the back of our cell hummed more loudly. He sounded like angry bees. I hoped he wasn't going to strangle us in our sleep. Not that I could sleep.

"Ask to send a message to her," Calev said.

I rubbed my temples. "We did. They won't. But I'm going to try again. Guard!" I called out, heading to the door. "He has a message for Pearl of the Desert's handmaiden, Meekra. This is her cousin, Radi."

Radi put a hand over his heart and smiled tentatively. He blinked silver raindrops from his thick, black eyelashes.

The middle-caste guard ambled over. "Fine. Fine. What is

this message? You better not be wasting my time. The others will never let me hear the end of it."

"We're telling the truth. This is important."

"He really is Meekra's cousin?" Respect and not a little awe flavored the guard's question. That would work to our advantage.

"She is very close to his branch of the family." I was lying almost as well as Oron. "If she finds out Radi is here, she'll definitely want to talk to him."

"Why are you just now mentioning this?"

I gave him my best glare. "We told the other guards."

The guard looked at his boots, kicked the bottom of the door.

"What can I tell you to persuade you to send the message?" Radi cocked his head.

The guard's puffy eyes flicked up. "Where was she born?"

Radi winced, then smoothed his face with a hand. "Akhmim."

The guard lowered his head and stared at Radi like he could somehow see through him. "I'll send a boy with a word. You better be telling the truth. What do you want the message to say?"

"That her cousin Radi has been wrongfully imprisoned and he knows something that will help her lady ease the kyros's worry about Jakobden."

"I doubt the boy will even get through, but fine, fine. I'll send it." With a nod, the guard ambled away, waving a hand to a stablehand wandering through the training fields.

I squeezed Radi tightly. "Thank you."

His smile warmed me even more than his body.

The guard waved a boy over and bent to speak into the messenger's cherubic face. The boy took off at a run.

Calev and I traded a look. It wasn't much to hang our hopes on, but it was something.

∼

Hours passed and the rain finally let up. Radi and I sat in the back of the cell, in the corner opposite that humming madman.

"Is this all right?" I set my head on Radi's shoulder.

My right eye kept twitching. I was so tired. Too tired to sleep. I couldn't stop staring at the far gates leading to the city, straining to see that messenger boy or a woman who looked well-dressed enough to be a handmaiden in the royal household.

"Of course, it's all right." Radi's voice rumbled in his chest. His knobby hands rested on his thighs and his breathing was a little uneven.

"Are you feeling sick?" It wouldn't have surprised me. This wasn't exactly a kyros's tent out here in the chill and wet and knowing we could be put to death at any second.

"No. I feel great. Considering."

I sat up, the ground wet under my palm, and looked into his face, at his crooked tooth and lopsided grin. "You're not breathing right."

He pinched his lips together. "I have a beautiful girl practically in my lap. How do boys usually breathe in these situations?"

The skin over my collarbone prickled. "I...I don't know."

I froze, not wanting to move. Scared to move and do something wrong. Something to make him stop thinking I was beautiful or I don't know… I felt like a sail tie that had been unwound and left to fly in the wind. I might break free of the knot and soar into the clouds. I might lash someone in the face. I might fall into the sea and drown.

A final drop of rain rolled down my cheek. Radi touched it, too rough at first, then easing. He dragged it across my face, then cupped my chin.

"May I kiss you?"

"Now? In prison? When my sister is dying?"

"It's terrible. I'm sorry. I'm terrible."

The world wasn't storming anymore, but my heart and mind were still being thrashed by worry and fear and anger and frustration. I suddenly wanted the heat of his lips on mine and the tiny, brief relief of knowing someone was right there beside me in this storm.

"Please do," I said.

"Please kiss you?"

"Yes." Tears welled in my eyes, hot and blurring Radi's face.

Gently, he set his peaked upper lip against mine, then his slightly chapped lower one. The chill went out of me and left me so, so warm. He pressed lightly, just once, then pulled back.

I wanted to say *Thank you* for being here for me, for helping me and risking everything for a person you just met. But I could only manage to say, "Now *my* breathing is uneven."

"Radi." Calev's voice rode across the air.

Radi shot to his feet, leaving me in a heap on the ground. "Calev ben Y'hoshua."

I got up, anger warring with curiosity.

Calev stood in his cell, arms crossed and face cloudy. "If we escape this, we will need to talk."

"Yes. Of course," Radi said, his cheeks going dark.

I smiled sadly. I was blessed to have a brother in Calev. He wouldn't be too harsh with Radi. He was only protecting me. As long as he didn't get too carried away...

A bright shape came over the hill from the city. A woman. The messenger boy trotted by her elbow.

"Calev. Look!"

The guard approached a woman—*Meekra, maybe?*—and he gave the woman a small bow. She was older than Kinneret, but not by much, and she wore a fine, black kaftan and a pink sash. Black hair flowed over a shoulder, hair like Radi's. When the guard pointed to our cell, her smile—lopsided like Radi's—slid off her face. She slipped a small bag to the guard, a coin to the boy, then turned right back around and left.

"Wait!" I called out.

The guard hurried over and banged his dagger's hilt against the bar. "Hush, girl. You'll get your food portion soon enough."

"I'm not hungry. I—"

The guard leaned so close that I could smell the spiced chicken he'd eaten earlier. "Trust me. Hush."

Radi and I gave Calev a loaded look and we settled back into our corner.

"Did she pay him off? What's going to happen?" I asked Radi like somehow he would know.

His lips came close to my ear, sending a shiver over my neck. "She definitely paid him some coin. But I don't know what for."

I squeezed my hands, pulling my skirt into my fists. "I guess we'll have to wait. I'm not good at waiting."

"No one is, are they?" Radi's gaze drifted over my face like he was trying to figure me out.

"I guess not."

᠆

Three guards brought flatbread into the cells. I took one, knowing I'd need my strength no matter what happened, and worked my mouth around it, trying to soften it enough to take a bite.

Radi frowned at his piece and turned it over. He must've been lucky enough to avoid stale food until now. I hated I was the reason he was eating it now.

The madman stopped humming. I turned, thinking he'd be eating, but he was staring at the door.

"Little birdies may fly," he whispered in a rasping voice. "Little birdies. Little birdies."

I choked on my bread. "Radi. The door. The guard left it unlocked."

"Come on." He dropped his portion, heading to the front of the cell.

I picked up the bread, tucked it in my sash for later, and followed.

The guards both had their backs to us, eating a much better meal.

Calev stood by his own door. He reached out a hand and pushed it open with a slight creaking noise. His was unlocked too. Flinching at the sound, he eased out of his cell. The people in with him just stared at the guards.

I opened our door and we took two steps. Shutting my eyes for a second, I prayed no one would say anything. My sandal caught on the cell door's frame. Heart tripping, I grabbed the bars, my breath leaving me in a gasp. Radi touched my back in support.

The middle-caste guard who'd taken the coin from the woman laughed loud and smacked the other one on the shoulder. He met my gaze with those puffy eyes of his, and my lungs froze. With a word, he could have us killed for trying to escape. But he gave a nod no one would notice except us and went back to his joking and eating and keeping his friend from turning.

We joined Calev and hurried into the shadows cast by the walls and highlighted by the moon. I swore he'd aged a year in a day.

"Ideas on what to do now, sister?"

I set my forehead on his shoulder for a second. "Act like we're supposed to be walking through these training fields and into the city instead of escaping?"

We walked as fast as we could without being noticed, thankful for the dark and dripping weather that camouflaged our shapes and our noise.

"So that was Meekra?" I asked as we passed through the back gates. Every guard gave us a questioning look. One started to call out a question, but we slipped into the city's darkness before he could sound the alert to our presence.

"I guess," Radi said.

"You knew she was born in Akhmim?"

"No. I guessed. It's a town near here."

"I doubt you guessed right," Calev said, not unkindly. "I'd bet she was only helping us out despite your error. Her mistress seems very open-hearted. It wouldn't surprise me if the woman at her side was the same."

I didn't care who helped or why. I just wanted to get out of this city and back to Kinneret with Calev and maybe Radi too since I doubted he could return to his family's cart. With every quick step, I glanced over my shoulder, just knowing there'd be fighters coming at us, ready to lock us back up or kill us on sight.

11
CALEV

On this side of the city, things were quiet. So different from the opposite side of Akhayma, where I'd lost the agreement and my only chance to show Father I could be the man he hoped I could be. I gritted my teeth, wishing more than anything that I could go back and do everything over again, the right way.

Canals gurgled as we passed through an area of dark, quiet tents. A man snored like a congested camel and a child called for his mother. In the market, tables were all folded up and put away. The sounds and smells of earlier had been washed away by the night's chill air, the sage and dust smell of the desert not so far away. We stopped near one of the booths that served as a home too, its striped walls gently lit from within.

Radi eyed the front door—slats of wood in a frame set over fabric lengths matching the walls. "I have to tell my cousin what's going on."

"But you're going to come with us, right?" Avi's admiration of this Radi colored her voice. "They'll find you here."

"I…guess I do have to come with you. Unless we hear something from Meekra."

"Could she manage to have you pardoned?" I asked.

"Anything is possible, I suppose." Radi slipped through the door.

We waited in the near dark. My ears strained to hear soldiers shouting that we'd escaped or dogs braying and on our scent. But so far there was nothing but the normal city sounds.

"Do you hear anything?" Avi grabbed the front of my tunic, her eyes bright and scared.

I cupped her hands with mine. "No, but—"

Noise exploded from the back of the city.

I ripped Radi's door open, sending the interior woven flaps fluttering. "They know. We need to go. Now!"

His family blinked and spoke rapidly in the desert tongue, handing him a bundle and shoving him toward us.

We took off down the street, Radi leading. Horses' hooves pounded the ground behind us.

"We'll never outrun them," I said.

"This way." Radi jerked my arm and I pulled Avi along as we sidled into an alleyway.

It was dark as the pitch Kinneret used to seal her boat. "What now?"

"Hopefully, they'll go past us," Radi whispered.

Avi bunched her hands and pressed them to her mouth. I put an arm around her and kissed her head, hoping to settle her down so they wouldn't hear the caste bells shaking on her clothing. Thankfully, Radi wasn't wearing any. He must've been purely of the desert blood.

The sounds grew louder. We huddled farther into the tight space between the tents. No noise came from the tents, so these must've been used as shops only during the day hours. The scent of oiled wood and a damped fire told me the one to our backs was a carpenter's place.

"No one's in there." I jerked my head at the tent. "Can't we slip under the wall and hide?"

"That's a big offense," Radi said. "If we're found in someone else's place, we will definitely be hanged. They take crime seriously here."

"It didn't seem to keep my attackers from stealing my things."

"Crime has increased. Because of the kyros. He raised taxes. Some of the low-castes and even a few middle are feeling the squeeze, so to speak."

The horses' pounding and the soldiers' voices rolled closer still. Then they were passing us, slowing, talking. One horse knocked against the carpenter's shop and shook the tent's posts and lines, pushing us.

Avi gasped.

The soldiers went quiet.

My heart beat against my temples, and I held Avi's fingers tight. Heat poured down my chest. Radi swallowed loud enough for me to hear.

Feet crashed to the ground. Someone had dismounted. Footsteps approached, grit crunching under boots.

Radi waved to us. He wanted Avi to wiggle deep into the alley of cloth walls, but there wasn't any room. The carpenter's place came together with the neighboring tent. Was there a passageway between the walls of striped wool?

I lifted a foot, trying not to scrape the ground, and nodded to Avi. She held my wrist with her cold fingers, clutching to me like her life depended on it. As if I could save her. But I couldn't. I could only follow Radi and hope we weren't heard.

At the spot where the tents came together, Radi pressed a hand out. It was so dark. I could only just now see more than the white stripes of the walls and the rough shape of Avi and Radi. There was the pale yellow of Radi's sash and the light streaming from the street where they were searching for us.

A man shouted and rushed into our hiding place. Avi pushed against me. Radi heaved himself through the tiny opening between the tents.

I spun and tried to help Avi through, but large fingers hooked my shoulder and arm and yanked me backward. Avi came with me and we landed in a pile at the soldier's feet, my hip hitting the ground sharply and Avi swearing and sounding like her sister. Radi hadn't been found.

The warriors hauled us out of the alley, not saying a word, features hard under their shining helmets. The middle-caste guard who'd left our cell doors open was nowhere to be seen. He probably fled with that money as soon as he could get away from the others.

An Empire fighter with a long face tugged my arms behind me and lashed them together with twine. The rope bit into my skin as he looped a knot over the saddle and began trailing me along like I was a prisoner of war. An enormous, bearded warrior bound Avi up, tying her to another mount.

Would this be it? After all we'd been through?

Kinneret would die without us there to say goodbye. Avi and I would hang or be whipped until dead, whatever horror the unpredictable kyros decided we deserved.

My legs were filled with lead weights and if I hadn't been tied to a horse, I would've crumbled to the ground.

They herded us back toward the Kyros Walls. At least Radi had escaped. I didn't know where he'd go. They'd probably know him by sight. Maybe they wouldn't bother going after him for such a minor infraction. It seemed Avi had been the one to really break the rules.

Avi tried to walk closer, but the fighters edged their horses between us, hooves inches away from our sandaled feet.

I couldn't stop thinking about Kinneret. Worry ate at me, biting here, gnawing there. I'd be nothing by the time I escaped again, if I ever had the chance. They wouldn't have to kill me. I'd die from fear for her.

They brought us to the main tent even though it was full night and no one seemed to be around. Inside, Avi and the warriors passed hands over the Holy Fire bowl while I went to my knees to wait, showing respect in advance.

Seren, Pearl of the Desert, slipped from a back room and into view. I should've studied her gaze for some kind of hint as to what she planned to do to us, but I couldn't stop imagining Kinneret and the sickness chewing at her bones.

Hands pushed my head down to bow lower, like Avi already had.

When we were allowed at last to stand, Seren frowned, studying me. The woman I believed to be Meekra, her handmaiden, came up beside her.

"The Holy Fire gave me an idea about your Kinneret tonight," Seren said. "So I couldn't let you leave. Not yet."

Invisible arrows pierced my heart. My breath stuck in my throat. I glanced at the Holy Fire bowl near the door. Its blue-orange Flame shimmered as if it knew we were talking about inspiration, all the blessings given to those the Fire chose.

"Is she..." My tongue couldn't create the horrible word—*dead*.

Her eyes seemed to tip downward at the edges, her lips going into a frown. "She may be soon."

Snakes slithered over my heart and I fisted my hands. "Can I save her?"

"I don't know. But I know you won't make it if I don't help you."

"So you believe my story about the agreement and Old Farm and the thieves?"

"I do. The Fire told me I need to send you home with a new agreement marked with Kyros Meric's personal sigil. I'm not sure how to make that happen though."

"The kyros still doesn't believe me." I didn't think it was a good idea to point out the fact that he obviously didn't believe the Fire had told her anything either. Or she hadn't told him for some reason.

"He may listen to me if I...put the idea in his head properly," she said.

I nodded.

She began to twirl a piece of green wool she had tucked into her sash. It looked like a piece of the clothing people wore in the mountains beyond the desert and I wondered what it meant to her.

"Take them back to the cells," she said, her gaze faraway. Meekra's mouth opened like she wanted to argue, but Seren held up a hand. "I have a plan."

THE CELL DOOR clanked shut and we were imprisoned again. Seren's guards sent the rest away and took up positions to watch us through the night.

We were left in the dark to wonder if tomorrow would mean Seren's success and our freedom, or her failure and our death.

12

AVI

The sun rose as I wiped tears off my face.

Sister, I'm trying to get him home to you. We're trying.

I still didn't regret coming. I couldn't have stayed there and watched her waste away. But nothing had gone as planned.

Seren's guards—the big man with the beard, the one with a face like a horse, and the thin one who'd captured us in the city—took us from our cell and brought us to a tent near the stables.

Bows, yatagans, and axes lined one wall. Two long tables crowded the front of the room. The man who'd been at the kyros's side when I'd seen him earlier stood near two other soldiers.

He crossed his arms and his gray eyebrows drew tightly together. "The Holy Fire gave my kyros an idea last night."

My knees shook. I tried to take a deep breath to keep from

falling over. Meekra wasn't here. No Seren either. We were doomed.

"He said," the general continued, "the Fire told him it was in the Empire's best interest to believe your story and send you on your way with your agreement approved."

I was a drowning girl suddenly pulled out of the waves. Air whooshed into my lungs, bringing me to life. We had a chance! A chance to save Kinneret!

Calev rushed to hug me, his hands sticky with nervous sweat.

"If you'll give my scribe the details," the general said, "all will be put in order. You're welcome to send your words of thanks to my kyros. Only one as strong in the royal blood could be so blessed as to hear so much from the Fire."

It had been Seren's blessing though, not Kyros Meric's. Well, it wasn't our secret to tell. I didn't much care who had done what, as long as we got out of here fast.

"Further, my generous kyros has decided to give your new amir two fine horses as a gift for his new appointment. You may return quickly to his service on these mounts." He nodded toward the door where the opening showed a yellow horse with a black mane and a full ebony mare with a beautiful star on her nose. Beside them, Arrow stomped her front hoof to get some attention. The chairman's horse, the one Calev had ridden here, nuzzled Arrow familiarly.

I pressed my hands into my face. I'd never been so relieved.

"Please thank Kyros Meric for his outstanding generosity," Calev said. "Please let him know we are in awe of his blessed ideas, and though I am Old Farm, I hold the highest respect for his path in life."

His blessed ideas? Humph. He'd taken credit for Seren's gift from the Fire. Then again, maybe that's how she'd wanted it. I wondered how she'd managed the trick.

As we mounted and thanked Seren's men for loading our packs with water, blankets, dried figs, and barley cakes, Meekra walked up.

"I see our kyros decided to let you go." There was a little spark to her eyes.

I leaned over in my saddle to speak close to her ear. "How did Pearl of the Desert do it?"

"How she always does. By waiting until he prays over the Fire and making suggestions as to what he, as the most blessed and rich in royal blood, must be hearing from the Fire."

Her lips turned down. I could tell she wanted to say more, to say the kyros was an arrogant fool who ate up praise before he tasted it for truth, but of course, that would be treason.

"Have you seen my cousin Radi since last night?" she whispered.

My heart cinched. "No. He escaped. I think."

Meekra looked over her shoulder. "If you see him on your way out of Akhayma…"

"I'll send you a rock dove as soon as I can."

"With…indirect language?"

Ah. She needed me to speak in code. He must not have been pardoned as of yet. "Can't Pearl of the Desert do something for him?"

"If we can find him, we'll protect him. But if the kyros's men find him first, we may not have a lot of options."

The gray-haired general stalked out of the tent and handed the new agreement to Calev, who bowed from his saddle.

I cupped my hand at Meekra's ear. "I'm glad we have Pearl of the Desert to help the Empire."

"Yes. Not all our leaders are merciful. We are indeed blessed to have Pearl of the Desert. Without her as kyros's wife, our city would be a different place." Meekra touched a letter tucked into her sash and smiled sadly. "She gives everything for her people."

"Tell her we love her for it."

"I will, Avigail Raza." Meekra pressed my hand between hers and gave Arrow's hind end a slap to send me off behind Calev.

"Come, Avi!" Calev's face was hopeful as he wrapped the two new horses' leads around one hand and tightened his legs around his father's mount. All I wanted in the world was for that hope to be fulfilled. All I wanted was to see Kinneret and him, smiling on their wedding day. All I wanted was home.

13
CALEV

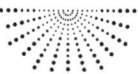

The horses couldn't go fast enough. I'd have slowed a little for Avi if she showed signs of needing it. So far, she was as driven to get to Kinneret as I was, shouting at Arrow, cheering the mare on. Prayers flowed from my mouth, a constant stream of *please please please*.

Hold on, love, I said in my mind, hoping somehow Kinneret would hear me. *I'm coming, love.*

I squeezed the reins, remembering the musky scent of the henna on my hands, the henna she'd painted on my skin. Shivers rolled over my arms and back. Her light touch. The tease in her eyes. The shift of her hips under the ivory cloth of the Intended ceremony clothing. I called memories up to make her strong in my mind. The courage in her face when she commanded the Tuz Golge. The moment she moved the very sea itself.

You're strong, love. Stay strong, love.

What was I going to do when I arrived? I couldn't save her. I didn't know anything about healing.

Avi glared at me over Arrow's head, determination blazing out of her eyes. She believed my presence would help Kinneret. I had no choice but to latch onto that faith.

The sandy plains and high, flat reaches of the hammadas gave way to the Greening's grasses and rolling hills. Stopping only when we couldn't stay on our horses without toppling over, we raced past the huddled villages, zipped between spice traders' caravans, and rounded clutches of pilgrims on their way to visit the heart of the Empire and the silver basin where the Holy Fire was lit every quarter.

∼

AT KINNERET'S new home by the docks, Oron sat, head in his hands. I slid off my horse, legs aching, to help Avi down. She slapped my hands away and pushed her hair out of her sweating face.

"Go. Go!" She waved at the blue door.

Oron looked up. A smear of dirt marred his chin. Red, puffy skin circled his big eyes.

I didn't wait to hear news. I pushed the entrance open, not knowing if I would find my life or death. Hers and my own.

Sunlight fell through the square window and onto Kinneret's ashen face.

Her lips were slightly parted and chapped. Her hair lay across her striped pillow, thin, and without its usual curl. I kneeled by her simple bed and swept her hand into mine. Her fingers were hot.

My heart jumped. *Alive.* She was blessedly alive.

Her eyes opened. "Having an adventure without me, hm?" she croaked. "Is this revenge for the time I went port-hunting and left you at home?" A smile bent her mouth.

I lay my head on her chest, keeping my weight back. She was on fire with fever. Her skin seared though her clothing. I breathed in the smell of stale linens, sweat, and green herbs used for healing teas.

"How are you?" I turned my head to look into her face, my fingers unsteadily holding hers.

"I've been better."

I tried to laugh. "I imagine."

She winced like something pained her, so I sat up, easing away.

"Don't go," she whispered, closing her eyes. She reached a hand around the back of my neck and let it sit there. Her chest moved in a deep breath. "I want to enjoy you as long as I can."

Tears blurred my vision. "You're not going to die."

"If I do, don't let anyone kaptan Ekrem's full ship but Avi or Oron. Swear to me." Her fingers tightened on my neck.

I shrugged. "I heard that new fighting sailor was pretty good. What's his name?"

She moved like she was about to sit up. "That idiot?"

"Settle down. I'm only teasing."

"Evil."

"It's your fault. I used to be a good boy."

Her eyes were slits, watching me. "What fun is being good?"

Oron walked up, hands clasped in front of him. His chin brushed my elbow as he leaned in to lift, then kiss Kinneret's free hand. "I claim at least some of Calev's moral ruin. You must admit I've had a part to play in the drama."

Kinneret laughed weakly as we helped her sip some tea

Oron took from the side table. The steam circled her head and made her look like a spirit.

Someone knocked.

Avi opened the door, biting her lip. "Your father's here, Calev."

The muscles around my jaw tensed. Of course he couldn't wait to hear about my duty. He'd think it was every bit as important as Kinneret. Maybe even more so.

Like he'd read my mind, he leaned in and said, "Talking to me won't change her condition, my son."

Giving Kinneret a pained look, I squeezed her hand, then joined my father in the blazing sun.

He unrolled the new agreement, brow furrowing. "This isn't the original." His eyes threw darts at me.

"No. I was robbed. In Akhayma. But this one has the kyros's sigil. It's legitimate."

Reading it over, he mumbled to himself, long beard shivering as he said the words under his breath. He rolled it back up. "It's fine. But tell me, what did you do wrong to be attacked wearing an Old Farm sigil ring and with the funds to stay in a safely located establishment at every stop? I did speak to Serhat."

I swallowed as Oron came out of the house.

"Is Serhat well again then?" I asked.

"Yes" Father's gaze held me down. "Now answer my question."

"I stayed in a terrible place because I was an idiot. Some men put gray plant in my food and robbed me."

Father stiffened. "Calev ben Y'hoshua. What were you thinking?"

Oron barked a laugh, though the sound didn't hold half his

normal enthusiasm. "Most likely he was thinking it'd be nice to forget you and yours for a while."

Father's look could've competed with the desert heat. He glanced at my hand and his mouth dropped open. "Where is your ring?"

"They took that too," I said.

His temper was going to get the best of him and mean the worst for me. He was going to deny my request to be the next chairman, take me completely out of the council's vote. Then what would I be for Kinneret? If she survived.

Father's face softened. "She is strong. She may live."

I glanced over my shoulder, not wanting Avi to hear Father's brutal honesty.

Oron touched my arm. "Avi's inside still. She can't hear us."

I nodded. "Can you wait to be angry with me?" I asked Father quietly, feeling like a child but knowing I had to ask it of him. I needed mercy.

His large hands covered my shoulders. "Yes. There will be consequences, but…"

Oron pushed his way into the conversation. "But you have a soul so you won't annihilate his future while his Intended sits on Death's door?"

Father's arms dropped to his sides. "Exactly so, Oron No Name."

There was a shout from the docks. It was Serhat, tall and blonde and pointing at an approaching dhow. The boat's triangular sail dipped in the wind as it came into the harbor.

A Kurakian woman in bright blue stepped onto the dock as Avi roared out of the house.

A light filled my chest and lifted the weight from my aching legs. I ran toward the water. It was Kania Turay, Kinneret's wise aunt.

"Aunt Kania!" Avi ran down the slope and crashed into her mother's sister.

"Ah, ah. Dear one." Kania stroked her niece's braid. "I will do what I can."

∼

A DAY PASSED in a whirl of bruising herbs Kania brought from the red dirt of Kurakia. The house smelled green and sticky.

"She isn't soaking it in," Kinneret's aunt whispered in my ear. "You must warm her up and get her to take the healing. To accept it."

I felt cold even though the room was stifling. "I don't know how."

Kania patted my hand, then ushered Oron and Avi from the room. "You will," she said over her shoulder. "You have a certain magic of your own, a magic between you."

She seemed so sure, yet doubt plagued my mind.

I sat on the very edge of the bed and rubbed Kinneret's arm. She did feel stronger now. The muscles under her brown skin weren't just wasted strings like yesterday. They'd plumped back up and there was a healthy warmth emanating from them. But it wasn't enough. Death breathed down her face, robbing it of color. I was going to lose her.

"Kinneret." I said her name like a prayer. "Kinneret." The sounds whisked over my lips, soft and sure. My love for her was the only thing I was truly sure of. "Kinneret."

Her eyes stayed closed as they had for hours. She breathed shallowly, like she'd stop at any second.

"Please wake up. Do you feel the good medicine in your blood? Your aunt put it there. You have to…let it in." I touched her collarbone, her neck. The skin there was too cold. It made me shiver.

With no idea what I was doing, just following the powerful tug I always felt to get nearer to her, I climbed onto the bed and lay directly on top of her. It was probably stupid. I was probably hurting her, but the pull—this was what my heart was telling me to do.

"Am I hurting you? Is this helping?" I propped myself on my elbows, my hands in her hair, my thumbs on the pulse in her temples. Smoothing my palms once down the sides of her head, I breathed warm air over her mouth.

She inhaled, moving me upward.

"Kinneret? Relax. Let the herbs do their work. Let your aunt's magic beat this. You can let her medicine fight. You don't have to fight. Let down your guard." I would be here always and I'd never act like such a careless idiot again, risking those I loved.

And stars, how I loved her.

She was so strong. She'd never once stopped fighting in life. Asking her to give in to the medicine and her aunt's magic, asking her to stop fighting—this was an impossible thing to ask. She'd fought her way from what others called a low-caste salt witch to being one of the most respected kaptans on the Broken Coast. Nothing had ever been given to her. Fighting was as natural to her as breathing.

"Calev." My name was nothing more than a whisper on her peeling lips. Invisible blades cut my heart at the longing in the sound.

"I'm here. I won't leave again."

She made a humming noise and shifted her body under me. Was it my imagination or was her skin warming, her temperature becoming more even?

Please let her live. She has so much more to do. I need her. Please, I prayed silently.

Her pale, blue eyes fluttered open. "Calev?" She blinked and her eyes widened. "You're really here?"

"I am."

"I thought I was dreaming." Her chest rose in a deep breath, a good breath.

"I dreamed of you while I was in Akhayma." My face flushed at the memory, and I hated myself for thinking like *that* while she was so sick.

"Tell me. About the dream." Her eyes drooped shut.

I swallowed. "I think the night of our Intended ceremony inspired it."

One eye opened, just a little. A smile curved her right cheek. "Tell me everything."

"You're too ill for…all of that."

"All of that."

"Yes."

She breathed deeply again and the color of her forehead, cheeks, and neck warmed to a nice flush. She looked at me. "I think I'm feeling better."

"It's your aunt's herbs. Her magic."

"It's yours too."

"I don't have any of that."

She moved and I slid to the side so she could lift herself to her elbows. She coughed, and I leaned to get her cup of water. With a small shiver, she took the drink and finished it all. With the edge of the cup, she drew a line down my neck, then my chest.

"Oh, yes you do," she said, her voice hoarse.

I kissed her smooth forehead, my muscles easing. "Please tell me you're finished trying to die." She really was feeling better. Hope rushed through me like wind through a field of ripe barley, pushing me, tugging me along its path.

"For now." She smiled up at me. "I need a bath."

I sat up and she did too, hanging her legs over the side of the bed as if she'd not just been at death's door.

I couldn't seem to stop smiling. Was this really happening? I was afraid to be happy. I ran a hand over her thin forearm. Her skin was oily and smelled like her aunt's house in Kurakia, green and biting and spicy.

She lifted a lock of her hair and sniffed. "Definitely a bath."

"I could help," I choked out, trying hard to contain myself.

Avi knocked and swung the door open. Her top teeth held her lip. "Aunt says you're feeling better."

I looked at the shuttered window, then at Kinneret, who shrugged. Kania just knew things.

"I am," Kinneret said, and a laugh bellowed out of me, happiness joining hope and throwing me right into pure joy.

Kinneret opened her arms and Avi ran into them, tears silvering her cheeks.

Oron and Kania came in laughing as Oron finished telling her something about his northern tastes in women.

"You have a powerful magic, Calev ben Y'hoshua," Kania said.

Avi moved away from Kinneret and put her hands on her hips. "I told you so."

I felt stronger than I ever had as I took Kinneret in my arms.

Maybe they were right. Maybe love was a magic all its own.

Never, ever again would I risk the magical life I had here with Avi, Oron, and Kinneret. I would live up to Father's expectations, and if I didn't, these amazing souls would still love me. I knew it as sure as I knew the beat of my own heart.

EPILOGUE

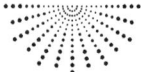

Kinneret

AMIR EKREM's full ship dipped over a wave and my stomach thrilled to feel the drop. The wheel moved under my hands, the wood polished and as ebony as Calev's eyes. The sea stretched out beyond us, purple and black and bursting with possibilities.

I shouted directions to a dozen fighting sailors who scurried to do as told. Lines were tied. Sails trimmed or angled. Ropes knotted to hold crates of Old Farm lemons that scented the deck and the salty sea air. The ship creaked as we rolled over another swell and I shook out my hair, letting it fly behind me like my own pennant.

Avi peered into the compass box, her movements light and quick.

Yesterday, a trader from Akhayma had brought her a

message from the boy she met there. A boy named Radi. His family had told the trader that Radi was gone from the capitol. He was safe. For now. This Radi fellow asked if she would go to the next Gathering. There, he would try to find her among the representatives from every noble clan, from every town and city, in the Empire.

Avi hadn't stopped smiling since.

But she hadn't heard the whole message. There were reports of Invaders attacking border towns again. Some said a drought had hit their western lands again and that war was on the horizon. I wondered if Kyros Meric could manage a war against those wild Invaders. From what Y'hoshua said, Meric wasn't wise like his father had been. Although so far Invaders didn't have the cannon us easterners had, they'd still give Akhayma and her people a load of nasty trouble. Deadly trouble for the new kyros and his new wife. I swallowed. Calev had told me about her. Under different circumstances, we could've been friends, he claimed.

Well, Avi didn't need to know the dark news about the Invaders. If it did come to war, Jakobden would be the last to feel it. There was plenty of sun to worry about that later.

"Are we on course?" I asked Avi.

"We are directly on course, Kaptan Kinneret. We'll be in Silvania in no time."

Silvania. Land of the proud, and too often, Jakobden and Old Farm's competition for port control.

"I don't like that smile, love," Calev said into my ear. His breath flew over my skin.

A pleasant warmth trickled down my neck and arm. "I'm only excited to trade with our neighboring country."

"You're excited about having the best ship in their port."

"It's a nice bonus."

The wind blew over my cheeks and fluffed the sails above us until they matched the blossoming clouds over head.

Avi watched the blue-gray sky's petals of mist open and close. "Is it going to storm?"

Oron took a bite of a plum. "I hope so. Watching Kinneret silently boast about her accomplishments is getting boring. When do I get a turn at the wheel, great kaptan?"

"Maybe right now." I turned to look into Calev's eyes and nodded toward the kaptan's quarters, my quarters.

Serhat ran a hand over her blond hair and waved to Avi, getting her to help teach a new sailor how to read the wind.

Calev met my gaze, his eyes hot. "There's definitely going to be a storm."

I gave Calev a teasing grin. "You're terrible at judging the weather."

He just glared and raised one eyebrow. "Am I wrong?" He wasn't talking about the weather.

Desire zinged down my body. "Oron can handle it," I said. "Can't you, Oron?"

Oron raised his chin and straightened his new tunic. The shapes were too tiny to be sure, but I guessed they were naked women. How he'd persuaded a fabric worker to create something like that…

"I'm insulted you'd even question it," he said.

I left him with the wheel and led Calev down the stairs and under the deck to my door. I remembered knocking on this door when Amir Mamluk was behind it. With Berker.

With a kick, the heavy oak door gave way. Calev slid hands around my middle and followed me inside. His fingers tripped over my sash and found skin where my shirt met my skirt.

I shivered and used a foot to slam the door shut on the old, sour memories of Berker and Mamluk, very ready to make new ones with the black-eyed, soul-lifting, luck-made-flesh love of my life.

Grab the next Uncommon World book, *Plains of Sand and Steel*, today! http://hyperurl.co/PoSaSUncommonWorld

ALSO BY ALISHA KLAPHEKE

Uncommon World Series

Waters of Salt and Sin

Fever

Plains of Sand and Steel

Forest of Silver and Secrets

The Edinburgh Seer Trilogy

The Edinburgh Seer

The Edinburgh Heir

The Edinburgh Fate

For a free Uncommon World prequel, visit alishaklapheke.com and get updates on Uncommon World news too!

Consider leaving a review for Fever on Amazon, Goodreads, or anywhere else you so desire. Reviews are important for everyone.

Plains of Sand and Steel
Uncommon World
Chapter One Sample

Seren

A hot, desert wind swirled around the dais, tugging at Seren's beaded kaftan and combing fingers through her jet hair as she stared down at the city. Her chest ached remembering her mother, who'd died when Seren was a baby, her father and sister—gone too—lost to Invader steel. But this city, it was her new home, and it eased that ache as she gazed at its people. Her people.

Akhayma looked a lot like a hand. Fingers of water slipped from the oasis and through the many canals. Stone walls cupped everyone in a dusty palm. The scene pulled a smile out of Seren. The grin would topple soon—Meric would see to that—but for now, the turned-up edges of her mouth held.

She savored the touch of happiness like a rare fruit as the pool's mosaics scattered moonlight between conversations.

"…and your grandfather shaped the steel that fought back the Invaders…"

"Your ancestors found this oasis and built Akhayma with their own hands."

Tonight, on this most special of nights, there wasn't any talk of business. Lovers didn't argue, and co-workers kept their talk for another time. Tonight, Seren's people laughed, wove stories, passed down details about *family*. That was what this was about.

Seren's smile broadened, lifting her cheeks and helping her stand beside the man she was too young to be married to and would never, ever have chosen for herself. Her father—the former High-General—had tried to keep her from this marriage, but the former kyros had ordered it. And not even generals said *No* to a kyros.

She stepped closer to Meric, hoping it wasn't too close. Sometimes he wanted to show her affection in public, but other times, no. Only ninety odd days into a marriage at seventeen, and she had little idea how to be a wife. Her smile wavered. She forced her lips up, afraid the light, easy feeling would be impossible to find if she lost it now.

"We should do this more often," she said, keeping that smile in place and ignoring Meric's narrowing eyes.

He coughed. "The Fire Ceremony?"

"Just rolling back the tents to open the city to the sky. It makes everyone more…talkative."

The varied languages floated through the night air like music. Coming back here, to the city of her birth, hadn't taken away the pain of losing her father, mother, and little sisters of course, but it lessened the ache in her soul. Akhayma had always been home.

Meric scowled at the Holy Fire bowl. Inside the large, silver basin, Flames danced in the lahabshjara leaves.

Beside them on the dais, the head of Clan Azjorr smoothed his black-striped kaftan. "Do you need another basket, Kyros Meric?" He gestured toward a servant clutching a hefty load of the emerald leaves.

Another cough tore through Meric. "What I need is to get on with this so I can rest."

The clan leader's cheeks darkened.

Seren apologized to the nobleman, using her black eyes to show her empathy, then spun to face Meric. "Let me call the physician."

"He never heals me."

Seren nearly pulled a muscle trying not to roll her eyes. Barir did help. When Meric let him. Her husband was older than her, but he was such a child.

"None of them fix anything." Meric glared in the general direction of the physician's home. Then, taking his position over the silver basin, he raised his high-pitched voice. "We gather here to honor the Holy Fire," he called out over the crowd.

He sounded like a bleating goat. Seren would've taken a goat over him any day. Goats didn't yell at anyone or insult good people. She imagined a goat's head in Meric's finely embroidered kaftan and had to stifle a laugh with her sleeve.

Despite Meric's distinctly lackluster delivery of the ceremony's opening words, the city quieted for their kyros.

"Giver of knowledge and wisdom," Meric continued, "weapon of our people, blessed and unrelenting. Holy Fire, grant us the Flame of your strength and invention. May ideas flicker from dreams into reality."

A warrior wearing a sweat-darkened military kaftan stepped out of the line. He was a scout.

A chill slid through Seren's bones.

The scout paused at the dais steps, his helmeted head bowed reverently.

Seren hurried over. "What's wrong?" she whispered as Meric went on bleating.

Standing on Meric's other side, General Adem eyed Seren. His gaze lashed out and she flinched a little. His eyes drew a line from her to Meric, who was still praying. He wanted her to wait until Meric finished speaking to talk. But this scout wouldn't be standing out of military line if everything was fine. Something was wrong and the Holy Fire would understand if there was an emergency. Seren clutched the scrap of mountain wool she kept in her sash, a bit of the skirt she'd been wearing when Invaders cut her family down.

"What is it, scout?" Meric snapped at the younger man.

The scout hurried up the stairs and approached Meric.

The wind rose, sand giving it little teeth. Seren raised the thin scarf hanging at her neck to protect her face and to mask any response she might have to the scout's report. An old trick of her father's.

Adem removed his silver helmet, his hair a close match, and inclined his head to listen.

"We spotted Invaders on the horizon," the scout whispered between Meric's continued coughing.

Seren shook her head. Surely she'd heard wrong.

"An army of them, my kyros," he said quietly to Meric. "Some on horseback."

Adem's mouth tightened. He kept an eye on those around them. "I was afraid of this, my kyros. When we first heard of their movement, I thought they were headed another direction, to invade lower Silvania instead. But…well, they will most likely strike Kenar for supplies after their journey from the West. They could conceivably cross our borders in two days.

Kyros, you must tell me what you wish to do." He stared at the Holy Fire bowl. "But please, finish the ceremony first."

Adem's face seemed to blur, his gray beard and sun-browned skin hazy. Seren blinked, the chill deepening, seeping into her blood, her heart. Meekra rushed to her side, and Seren took the handmaiden's slim fingers in her own. Despite her friend's kind touch, Seren's mind threw out memories of the Invaders' sharp eyes, their wide, steel weapons, the way they shouted when they killed like it hurt them to shed blood, but they loved it anyway. She'd known they'd return. It was why she prayed for ideas from the Fire, kept up her studies of Father's military scrolls, and trained in horse and bow daily.

"I must..." Meric's coughing doubled him over.

Chilled blood racing through her, Seren took Meric's arm and started him toward the stairs.

"But you must finish..." Adem started.

"What should we do, my kyros?" The scout twisted a hand around the hilt of his yatagan.

"He'll answer you as soon as the physician treats him," Seren said, hoping Meric *had* an answer.

General Adem addressed the city, and Seren watched over her shoulder as dark and light eyes both turned up to focus on him. "There is a military issue we must deal with immediately. Your kyros has blessed the basin, and you may come, one family at a time, to light your homefire sticks. May the Fire bless us all."

As Seren hurried Meric away, with their guards and servants around them, she said, "Call for your father, Meekra."

She didn't care that Meric thought the physician never helped. Meric was wrong. Barir knew several ways to calm this cough he struggled with day-to-day.

The Kyros Walls rose up beside them as they entered the courtyard and headed toward the main tent. Another gust of sand grated across Seren's bare forearms and the single bell tied around her head to hang between her eyebrows.

"And Cansu," she said to the long-faced guard who'd been kind since the day he was assigned to Seren, "you will go with Meekra. I don't like this weather."

The two rushed into the night while her other two guards and a handful of Meric's fighters followed Seren and Meric inside.

In the main tent, the moon bled through the ceiling's patterned weave. Light in the shape of blurry stars dotted the room. At the door dividing the main tent from Seren and Meric's personal chambers, the guards took up positions, relieving the men that had been there during the ceremony.

"Erol," Seren said, "Protect the back entrance to my chamber along with the others serving there now. Tell them nothing. I don't want anyone worrying."

Hossam, black hair more wild than normal, pushed the door back, the woven flaps too, and helped Seren get Meric inside. Erol sped past them, heading out the rear door of the bed chamber. Hossam gave Seren a quick bow, then left to join the other armed men and women in the main tent.

Another tight cough shook Meric. Seren worked the knot in his ceremonial phoenix sash, then threw it to the ground, trying anything to make him more comfortable. White skin ringed his mouth. He dropped to sit on the bed, chin down, hands splayed and covering the bedcover's calligraphy that spelled out his name and title. *Kyros Meric, the Eternally Victorious.*

Lying back on a tasseled pillow, he shut his eyes, gasping like a fish without water.

SAMPLE OF PLAINS OF SAND AND STEEL

Where was Barir?

Meric needed the physician now. Maybe Meekra and Cansu were having trouble getting to his quarters in the weather. What if a sandstorm hit right now?

Tears burned at the corners of Seren's eyes. Invaders. Sandstorms.

Meric *had* to be all right.

She didn't know how to take care of an Empire. Images of maps and lists of agreements—from Father's time as the old kyros's general—flickered through her head. Father had taught her a lot. But talking about leading was different from actually doing it. She wasn't the heir anyway. She didn't have any royal blood.

The whistling in Meric's lungs kept on, and he gasped more violently, his back arching at a painful angle. Seren couldn't stop shivering.

Barir walked into the room, tugging at his long, gray beard, his dark eyes worried. Meekra and Cansu trailed the physician like shadows.

Seren heaved a breath. "Please. Help him."

Meric's color was all wrong.

"I need to dose him with ka'ud," Barir said as he approached the bed.

Meekra tucked a curl of dark hair behind her ear, took her father's medicine satchel, and set it on the side table.

Cansu's throat moved in a swallow. His hand brushed the five high-caste bells on his sash as he joined the other guards outside the door.

Seren heard Adem's low grumble of a voice outside the door, probably asking for a report on the kyros's state.

"I'll tell him he's being treated," Meekra said.

Seren couldn't look away from Meric. The sudden hollowness to his cheeks. The hair hanging over his left eye. His kaftan rumpled under his arms and how he did nothing to fix it.

"Thank you," she said to Meekra.

Barir pulled a length of the rare, resinous wood from his bag and set a shallow dish on the bedside table. Praying quickly over the Holy Fire bowl in the corner, he lit the ka'ud with the Flames and arranged the smoking wood in the dish. Blue clouds billowed over the kyros. Barir listened to Meric's lungs, his head on his chest.

Meric's shifting legs stilled.

Something sharp and cold cut into Seren's heart and she reached for his hand. His fingers were too limp.

"Meric?" Her heart beat in her ears.

He didn't move. Didn't speak. His lips had gone blue.

Barir rose. "Pearl of the Desert, I don't want to tell you this."

She held her breath.

"Please forgive the bearer of bad news." His voice dropped to a hush. "The kyros is dead."

The buzz in her ears was deafening.

Meric, the man whose father saved her from the Invaders who'd killed her little sisters and father, the man who acted like a spoiled child one minute and a violent storm the next, Meric the Eternally Victorious, was dead.

Shaking so badly she could hardly stand, Seren positioned Meric's hands on his chest as was custom. He looked so much like his father had. Her own father's closest friend. Sweat bloomed across her forehead and chest.

No. It can't be.

Barir stared at her and moved his lips like he was about to say something.

"What should I do?" An invisible sandstorm tore at her thoughts, her heart. She gripped the edges of the bed to stay upright. In the corner, the Holy Fire's orange-blue fingers spread over emerald leaves.

"You should pray, general's daughter," Barir whispered.

"Now?"

"I've seen you pray, my lady." His mouth relaxed into a solemn line.

Seren was shaking all over. "Don't call me *my lady*. You've known me since I was a baby."

"You are the highest in the land as of now." Face grave, he nodded toward the Fire.

She went to the bowl and passed her hands over the flickering light. Bright heat tickled her palms. Her eyes fluttered shut, then open again. A familiar peace slid over her like a warm breeze on a chilly night, and her shaking eased. The small basin's copper surface reflected the orange-blue Flames. Barir stayed quiet.

Please, I need help, she prayed silently.

Holding both palms at an angle over the Fire, she took a deep breath. The skin between her eyebrows twinged and a warmth rushed through her heart, all the way to her fingertips.

A curl of Flame appeared in front of her face, hovering high over the bowl.

She gasped.

Barir said something quick and quiet under his breath.

Many prayed to the Holy Fire. Only a few in history were blessed with the Hovering Flame, the true light of invention and purpose.

The flesh in Seren's hands glowed with the intense shine of

the Holy Fire. Illuminated from within, bones showed under red skin as a vision burned into her mind.

The corners of the Empire shimmered into view. Places she'd traveled to with Father when he was still the High General. Far off towns and seas. Markets and boats. Laughing children. Men and women talking, some singing, some arguing. Light skin, darker skin, people from every clan in the plains and the border towns in the mountains where Father had taken the family when he retired.

Then Akhayma came into view.

A shadowy cloud churned in the sky beyond the walls. Above it all, a length of pure white linen wrapped itself around Meric's body. The storm near the walls shimmered, became men with wide weapons of steel, screaming and weeping as they swamped the city, more deadly than any storm. In the vision, Seren waved a hand and hid Meric's corpse in the night clouds. She took up his best kaftan—a kyros's kaftan, hemmed in silver phoenixes—and raised it above her head. The invading men blew into dust. *Kyros Seren!* the people shouted, suddenly smiling and holding their homefire branches. Their lights became the stars above the desert, and a calm covered Seren's panicking heart like a great, invisible hand.

The vision faded.

The thread of Holy Fire in front of her face unspooled and fell into its brother and sister Flames.

She faced Barir. The real world—along with its very real trouble—intruded as suddenly as an arrow from the darkness, piercing Seren's calm and bleeding it dry until she trembled again. All in the time it took to breathe in.

The things she'd seen...it had only been her imagination. She hadn't seen a vision. It was impossible. Wasn't it? The Fire had given her ideas before, but they'd been simple words and thoughts in her head, small things like the idea to free that kind-eyed young man from Old Farm and to hire the famed mercenaries of Silvania. It was odd enough to gain those ideas without royal blood, but actual visions? It just could not be. But…

"I saw something." It was like a stranger said the words. She felt detached from her own body.

Barir took a shuddering breath, the ka'ud smoke clouded around his black hair. "A vision. You had a vision." His hand went to his mouth.

She swallowed. "Maybe. I…" She was coming apart, her ears buzzing, the world spinning.

Suddenly she was in Barir's wiry arms, his graying beard brushing against her head and his shushing sounds in her ears like she was still a child.

"Do you want to tell me what you saw? It may help us all in this terrible moment. No one has seen a vision in the Fire in, one, maybe two, centuries." He held her away from him enough to look into her eyes. "You are blessed. Chosen."

Focusing on his face, the face she'd known as long as her own, Seren told him what she'd seen.

Barir's eyes sharpened. "The Invaders approach. Kyros Meric is dead, so General Adem will send for Varol, Meric's brother and heir of the royal blood. But you can't let that happen."

She'd only really heard one word. A name. Varol. She swallowed a bitter taste rising in her throat. "What?"

"General Adem will send the city into mourning. Invaders or not. He will. He is arrogant. That shroud you saw? That was the city mourning. The Invaders triumphed while we mourned."

The traditional mourning song slithered through Seren's head.

The soul is heavy,
Three days, three days,
Your shoulders are free,
Take up the weight of Death.
The soul is tired,
Three days, three days,
You slept through the night,
Give your sleep to the Dead.
The soul is starving,
Three days, three days,
Your table is full,
Give your food to the Dead.
The soul is heavy,
Three days, three days,
Your shoulders are free,
Take up the weight of Death.

Her people would be weakened. Her warriors weakened. Her adopted family weakened, and at the mercy of the merciless.

"But he can't force everyone to mourn," she said. "If everyone stops eating and sleeping, we'll be easy to defeat. He would know that."

"You saw yourself pushing the mourning away. Then you saw our city at peace. Seren. Pearl of the Desert." He used the title given to her when she was married to the kyros. "You must claim leadership of the Empire. You have been chosen."

"No. That's not…"

"Then how do you see it?"

"We must announce the death and tell everyone to wait until after the attack to mourn."

"And if we survive, which we won't, General Adem will call for Varol and he will become kyros."

She hugged herself. Meric's younger brother was so much worse than even Meric had been. The way he used people…

Father had saved a slave working for Varol. Because of the woman's skill with the horses, Father had paid for her apprenticeship with the stables here in Akhayma. She'd been raised to middle-caste before he retired. But she still carried Varol's scars. Thick, clawed fingers of raised skin striping her back and shoulders. Seren's stomach clenched.

General Adem's voice came through the door. "May I enter to see the kyros, Pearl of the Desert?"

"I…"

Barir whispered in Seren's ear. "I will claim the kyros has something that may be contagious. I will keep everyone away. That will give you time."

"Time for what?"

"Pearl of the Desert." Adem rapped on the door.

Barir put his hands on Seren's shoulders. "It will give you time to fight off the Invaders. Then, you can decide whether or not to embrace your fate."

"My fate? No. That can't be what I'm supposed to do."

"Why not? You are a general's daughter. You traveled with him. You learned from him."

"I'm not of royal blood. I'm not even fully desert blood. General Adem would never support me."

"He isn't fully desert either. Not many are."

"That doesn't matter," I whispered. "He's ruled by tradition. You've seen him. He worships the royal blood nearly as much as the Fire. And if he finds out I hid Meric's...condition, he'll have me beaten to death."

"The Fire showed you what to do. You know you trust in it."

"About this though...this is madness."

Adem knocked again. "I must insist to see my kyros."

Seren hugged Barir again. He kissed her forehead like she was Meekra's sister, another daughter.

"I'll keep everyone out," Barir said. "We can talk about the rest later. And my dear Seren." His eyes softened but were no less unblinking, his stare no less steady. "Fate rarely waits until we're ready. How many times would we say *No* in preparation for something great? Every time. We would never feel fully armed. You are more ready than most and you must believe you are enough."

Wisdom glinted in his eyes. But he wasn't right about this. There was no way he could be right about this. Mind humming, she followed him out of the room.

Shutting the door behind them, Barir bowed to Adem. "General, our kyros has contracted what I believe to be a contagious disease of the respiratory system. We must keep everyone out, except Pearl of the Desert, Meekra, Cansu, and myself since we have been in close contact already. We've all taken a ka'ud potion, so we may come and go without danger to others, but no one else should be risked. It could lead to an epidemic."

Seren bit her lip. They were lying to the highest ranking

military man in the city. To Meric's right hand. Cansu looked confused, but he held his tongue.

"It is...for safety," Seren said. "We must be very careful. Especially now that we're under attack. I will tell the rotating guards to keep all of this to themselves, and to make certain no one, including them, may enter the chamber."

Adem looked to the door, blinked. "Can you heal him?"

"I can't say yet. It is..." Barir glanced at Seren. "Too soon to tell."

Adem's body tensed beneath his armor, and his jaw sharpened—a warrior trained to absorb a strike when he had to. Though this blow had nothing to do with fists or steel. It was Adem's loyal heart taking the news that his beloved royal was seriously ill. Seren had never been close to Adem, but sympathy flooded her nonetheless.

"Fine," Adem said. "I will pray for our kyros and lead the troops as best I can until tomorrow when, Fire make it so, I may speak with our kyros for his final decision on what action to take."

With a curt bow to Seren, he spun on his heel and headed for the Holy Fire bowl at the main tent's door.

Meekra's eyes couldn't get any wider. "Should I go in with you, my lady?"

The guards and fighters standing watch shifted their weight, looking like lost children instead of people trained to kill.

"Yes, Meekra. We'll tend to the kyros." She waved, indicating Meekra should join her inside.

"I'll announce the quarantine to the criers so everyone will know to keep their daily supplications to themselves for the time being," Barir said before they left.

Seren turned, knowing the tears at the corners of her eyes

made her look too young to give orders. "Tell the scribe too. He must take hold of the business side of things while we...until the kyros is well."

"My lady." Barir bowed and held Seren's gaze for a heartbeat. "Remember, you are blessed."

Seren rushed into her personal chambers, wanting nothing more than to run away from the burden Barir's beliefs and her vision had stacked onto her shoulders.

Grab the rest of this novel today. http://hyperurl.co/PoSaSUncommonWorld

Lightning Source UK Ltd.
Milton Keynes UK
UKHW011831151221
395702UK00001B/249